Book II
The Shapeshifter
In the
Tales of Mulvyon

The Shapeshifter's Wrath

Tales of Mulvyon, Volume 2

Oscar Wayne

Published by Oscar Wayne, 2024.

This is a work of fiction. Similarities to real people, places, or events are entirely coincidental.

THE SHAPESHIFTER'S WRATH

First edition. October 21, 2024.

Copyright © 2024 Oscar Wayne.

ISBN: 979-8227796844

Written by Oscar Wayne.

Table of Contents

Chapter 1 1
Chapter 2 6
Chapter 3 15
Chapter 4 25
Chapter 5 41
Chapter 6 50
Chapter 7 59
Chapter 8 70
Chapter 9 84
Chapter 10 98
Chapter 11 106
Chapter 12 117
Chapter 13 132
Chapter 14 143

Chapter 1

As Lethiriel's figure disappeared into the dense greenery of the new lands, the group stood in silence, the weight of her departure settling heavily over them. The vibrant landscape that surrounded them, teeming with life, now felt more like a trap than a triumph. Kairos, Otona, and Gronkar exchanged uneasy glances, each of them feeling the pressure of the unknown.

Otona broke the silence first, pacing back and forth, her brows furrowed. "I don't like this," she muttered. "If Lethiriel knows something about the shapeshifter, why wouldn't she tell us? What is she really after?"

Her voice was sharp with frustration, and Kairos could tell she was on edge. It wasn't like Otona to be rattled, but the uncertainty of the situation—of Lethiriel's true motives—was eating at her.

"Doesn't matter," Gronkar replied gruffly, crossing his arms as he stared after Lethiriel's retreating figure. "We can't trust her. What we need is a plan."

Kairos remained quiet, absorbing their words as he mulled over their options. The weight of leadership pressed down on him harder than ever. They were standing at the edge of something monumental—these new lands, born of dark magic, were filled with both potential and danger. But where did they even begin? They had no clear direction, no understanding of what the shapeshifter was capable of, and the new lands themselves felt unstable.

He sighed, running a hand through his hair. "But where do we even start?" he asked aloud, more to himself than to the others. "We don't know where the shapeshifter is, and we don't even know if these lands will hold. Tythalor warned us that they were temporary, and there's no telling how much time we have before they fall apart."

Otona stopped pacing and looked at him, her expression softening. "You're right. These lands could collapse at any moment. And if

Lethiriel knows more about the shapeshifter than we do, we're already at a disadvantage."

"Which is why we shouldn't be standing around worrying about what Lethiriel's doing," Gronkar growled. "She's made her choice. We need to focus on the shapeshifter before it causes more damage."

There was a growing tension in their conversation, the weight of their uncertainty looming large. None of them knew what to expect in this new, fragile world. They were in uncharted territory, facing threats they couldn't predict, and the shapeshifter was a dangerous wild card in all of it. The thought of it lurking somewhere out there, hidden within the new lands, only added to their unease.

"We could follow her," Otona suggested, her voice uncertain. "See where she goes, try to stay one step ahead of her."

Kairos shook his head. "We'd just be chasing her without any clear direction. And if these lands really are unstable, we can't afford to waste time."

"So, what do we do?" Otona asked, frustration edging into her tone again. "We can't just wander blindly through the new lands hoping to stumble across the shapeshifter."

Kairos thought for a moment, the pieces slowly coming together in his mind. "There's a nearby elven settlement, not far from here. They might have information, maybe even resources that could help us. And..." He hesitated, glancing at Otona. "We might find out more about what Lethiriel is really after."

Otona's eyes narrowed slightly, but she nodded in agreement. "The elves would be our best bet. They might know something about the magic that created these lands, or the shapeshifter itself."

"Fine," Gronkar grunted. "But if they give us any trouble, I'm not playing nice."

Kairos allowed himself a faint smile, appreciating Gronkar's readiness for a fight even in moments like these. "We'll cross that bridge when we get there."

The decision was made. They wouldn't chase after Lethiriel, but they couldn't stay idle, either. They had to stay focused on their mission—finding and stopping the shapeshifter before it could cause any more harm. If that meant starting with the elves, then so be it.

Kairos turned his gaze to the horizon, where the new lands stretched out in all their unnatural beauty. The path ahead was uncertain, but he knew one thing for sure—they couldn't afford to lose momentum.

"We move at dawn," he said, his voice steady with resolve. "Let's see what the elves know."

With that, the group prepared to rest, knowing the real challenges were just beginning.

As the group gathered their belongings, preparing to leave for the elven settlement, a sudden tremor rippled through the ground beneath their feet. Kairos froze, the soft vibrations beneath the earth sending an ominous signal. He exchanged a wary glance with Otona and Gronkar, each of them instantly on high alert.

The once-lush landscape, now pulsing with latent magic, seemed to hum with life—an unsettling, chaotic life. The vibrant trees swayed unnaturally, and the earth itself appeared to breathe, as if the land was alive but fragile, teetering on the edge of collapse.

"What was that?" Otona asked, her voice tight with unease.

"I don't know," Kairos replied, clutching the medallion fragments in his hand. They pulsed faintly, the magic inside them responding to something in the new lands. He could feel it—a connection, as if the medallion was still tied to whatever force was shifting the world around them.

The ground trembled again, this time with more intensity. In the distance, they heard a strange sound—a deep, unsettling groan, as if the earth itself was twisting and reshaping. It was unnatural, like something ancient and powerful stirring beneath the surface.

"Feels like the whole place is ready to tear itself apart," Gronkar muttered, scanning the horizon with suspicion. His hand rested on his Warhammer, ready for a fight.

Kairos's mind raced, considering the possibilities. "The medallion... it's reacting to something. There's magic in these lands—Tythalor's magic—and it's unstable. We might not be alone out here."

Otona's eyes narrowed. "You think the shapeshifter is nearby?"

Kairos nodded slowly, though he wasn't certain. "It's possible. Or it could be something else entirely. But whatever it is, we need to stay alert."

The groaning sound echoed again, louder this time, and the ground shook more violently. The group instinctively huddled closer together, their eyes scanning the surroundings for any sign of immediate danger. But the landscape was still, deceptively quiet, save for the unnatural pulse of magic beneath their feet.

"We need to move," Kairos said, his voice firm. "This place isn't stable. We need to find shelter and figure out what we're dealing with."

Without hesitation, the group gathered their gear and started moving, their footsteps quick and deliberate as they sought a safe place to regroup. Whatever was happening in these lands, they had no intention of sticking around to find out. But one thing was clear: the new lands were far more dangerous than they had imagined.

As the group settled in a small clearing tucked between a cluster of rocks and newly formed trees, a sense of temporary safety enveloped them. The air was cool, and the distant rumblings of the unstable lands faded into the background. They had found a place to rest, but none of them felt fully at ease.

Kairos sat apart from the others, staring at the medallion fragments in his hand. The faint glow they emitted was a constant reminder of what they had left behind—and of the decision he had made to reject Tythalor's offer. Guilt gnawed at him, though he tried to push it down.

As their leader, he couldn't afford to dwell on doubts, but the weight of responsibility had never felt heavier.

Otona moved silently through the camp, checking her weapons and preparing for what lay ahead. She glanced over at Kairos, noticing the tension in his posture. "We'll find the shapeshifter, Kairos," she said, her voice calm but determined. "And when we do, we'll stop whatever it's planning. We didn't come this far to fail now."

Gronkar, sitting by the small fire they had built, nodded in agreement. "We'll crush it. Whatever it is, it won't stand a chance against my Warhammer. We just have to stick together."

Kairos looked up at his companions, grateful for their resolve. Despite the uncertainty and the growing danger, they were ready to face whatever came next.

"We will stop it," Kairos said, his voice steady. "For Mulvyon, for these lands, and for everyone who's counting on us."

As night fell, the group rested, but the air was thick with foreboding. The path ahead would test them in ways they couldn't yet imagine, and Kairos knew that their greatest battles were still to come.

Chapter 2

The sun had barely risen when Kairos, Otona, and Gronkar set out, their footsteps light but their hearts heavy. The new lands that had sprung up around them were exotic, vibrant, and brimming with life—but there was something deeply unsettling about them. Rivers now flowed through what had once been arid deserts, lush forests had risen where there had been barren wastelands, and strange creatures skittered in the shadows, drawn to the unstable magic that pulsed through the landscape. Every step they took felt like walking on a delicate balance, with the land itself ready to shift beneath their feet.

Otona led the way, her eyes constantly scanning the horizon, always alert to potential threats. As a ranger, she had a deep connection to the land, but even she couldn't shake the feeling of unease. The new life around them didn't feel natural—it felt forced, as if the magic had twisted the world into something it was never meant to be.

"There's something wrong here," Otona muttered, her voice low but firm. "This place... it doesn't feel right."

Gronkar grunted in agreement, his massive form bristling with tension. "It's unnatural. The magic that created this place. I can feel it in my bones."

Kairos walked a few paces behind them, silent and thoughtful. The weight of his decisions pressed down on him, heavier than the medallion had. He couldn't stop thinking about the medallion, the power it had unleashed, and Lethiriel's hasty departure into the new lands. Could they have stopped her? Could they have prevented all of this? He didn't have the answers, and that uncertainty gnawed at him.

"There's no point dwelling on the past," Kairos finally said, breaking the silence. "We made our choice. Now we have to deal with what comes next."

The group continued their journey in tense silence, their eyes fixed on the path ahead. The air was thick with the hum of magic, and every now and then, they would catch glimpses of strange creatures darting between the trees—creatures that hadn't existed in the old world. It was as if the land itself was alive, reshaping and evolving with every moment.

As they neared the outskirts of the elven settlement, the atmosphere changed. The chaotic energy of the new lands gave way to something more stable, more ancient. The subtle hum of elven magic lingered in the air, a stark contrast to the unpredictable forces they had felt earlier. It felt protective, as if the very land was warded by ancient spells, keeping the unstable magic of the new lands at bay.

"We're close," Otona said, her voice barely a whisper. "But the elves might not welcome us."

Gronkar chuckled darkly. "When do elves ever welcome anyone?"

Kairos sighed. "We don't have much of a choice. They might be the only ones with answers."

The group pushed forward, their eyes sharp and their senses on high alert as they approached the borders of the elven settlement. They could feel the weight of elven eyes watching them, though no one had made themselves known yet. The ancient power of the elves contrasted starkly with the chaotic magic of the new lands, reminding them that this world, too, had its own dangers.

As the group approached the outer edges of the scholar's boarders, they were greeted by the sudden tension of drawn bows. Elven warriors emerged from the tree line, swift and silent, surrounding Kairos, Otona, and Gronkar with precision. The air crackled with magic as the elves raised their bows, arrows notched and pointed directly at them. These were no ordinary guards; their eyes were sharp, their movements graceful.

The leader of the patrol stepped forward, his stance rigid, eyes narrowed with suspicion. His long silver hair flowed down his back, and his piercing green gaze landed directly on Kairos, sizing him up with cold precision. This elf was not a stranger to authority or danger, and his posture made it clear he would not hesitate to strike.

"You shouldn't be here," the elven leader said, his voice like ice. "These lands are not for outsiders to wander freely."

Before Otona could speak, she recognized the elf—Taflas, a well-respected warrior within the settlement and a close friend of her half-brother, Rhylar. This complicated things. Otona knew Taflas to be loyal to the elven cause, protective of his people, and not easily swayed. It would take more than a few words to convince him of their intent.

Otona stepped forward, careful not to make any sudden moves. "Taflas," she began, keeping her tone respectful but firm. "We seek information, nothing more. We mean no harm."

Taflas raised an eyebrow but didn't lower his bow. His eyes flicked briefly toward Otona, recognizing her immediately. "Otona," he said, his voice still cold but tinged with familiarity. "These are dangerous times. The magic that created those lands is dangerous. You walk in its shadow."

Kairos could feel the tension mounting. He tightened his grip on the remnants of the medallion, wondering if these elves saw them as the cause of all the chaos. He opened his mouth to explain, but Otona silenced him with a quick gesture.

"We are not your enemies, Taflas," Otona said, stepping forward with quiet confidence. "We've been fighting the same magic that created these lands. A shapeshifter was awakened when the new lands formed. It's a threat to us all, including your people. We need help to stop it before it does any more damage."

Taflas's expression remained hard, but a flicker of doubt passed through his eyes. He glanced at the other elves, and they exchanged uncertain glances. The creation of the new lands had shaken them as much as anyone, and they knew the balance of magic had been disrupted. But trusting outsiders, even one as familiar as Otona, was not a step they took lightly.

"The new lands are unnatural," Taflas said, his voice still laced with suspicion. "Born of dark magic. You travel with it, and it's dangerous."

Gronkar, standing just behind Kairos, muttered something about elves being too high-strung, but before he could say more, Otona shot him a silencing look.

"We didn't create this," Otona insisted. "We're trying to stop it. The shapeshifter is the real danger. If you don't help us, the consequences will reach far beyond these lands. This isn't just our fight, Taflas."

Taflas hesitated, his sharp eyes scanning the group. The elves, still wary, kept their bows raised, though there was a visible shift in their posture. Otona's words had struck a chord. The chaos of the new lands had shaken the elven community, and they understood the need to act—but trusting outsiders had never been part of their way.

Finally, Taflas lowered his bow, though his expression remained guarded. "Very well," he said, his voice measured. "I will take you to Finwe, our scholar. If anyone can help you make sense of this, it's him. But make no mistake—we will be watching you closely."

Kairos let out a quiet sigh of relief as the elves began to lower their bows. He exchanged a glance with Otona, grateful for her calm under pressure. Gronkar crossed his arms but remained silent, his expression dark.

As the group was led deeper into the settlement, the atmosphere shifted. The air grew calmer, more controlled, as if the magic within the elven village was designed to counteract the chaos of the new lands. Tall, elegant trees loomed overhead, their bark shimmering faintly with the touch of ancient runes. Elven structures, carved into the trees themselves, exuded a sense of timeless beauty, their spiraling staircases and arched doorways blending seamlessly into nature.

Taflas guided them to the heart of the settlement, where a grand, intricately carved tree structure stood. Its roots seemed to merge with the earth, and its branches reached high into the sky. Taflas gestured for them to enter.

"Finwe awaits inside," he said, his tone still edged with distrust.

Kairos, Otona, and Gronkar exchanged a final glance before stepping into the ancient building, hopeful that the elven scholar held the answers they desperately needed.

The inside of the tree structure was as breathtaking as it was otherworldly. The walls, formed by the living wood of the tree, twisted into intricate patterns, glowing softly with runes that seemed to hum with ancient magic. Golden light filtered through the cracks in the bark, casting a serene, almost mystical glow over the room. At the center of the space was a large, circular table made of the same tree, its surface etched with more runes, some of which pulsed with the rhythm of the earth.

Finwe, the elven scholar, sat at the far end of the room, his sharp eyes watching the group with a mix of curiosity and quiet wisdom. His silver hair flowed past his shoulders, shimmering like river water, and his long robes, embroidered with more runes, almost seemed to move of their own accord, as if they were connected to the magic around him. Though elderly, there was an undeniable sharpness to his gaze, a clarity that spoke of centuries of knowledge and experience.

As Kairos, Otona, and Gronkar entered the room, they felt the weight of Finwe's presence, a commanding yet gentle energy that filled the space. He motioned for them to sit, but his eyes remained locked on Kairos, as if he could see something within him that the others could not.

"Welcome, travelers," Finwe said, his voice soft yet commanding. "I know what you seek."

Kairos stepped forward, feeling a strange pull toward the elderly elf. Despite having never met, he felt a peculiar sense of familiarity, as if Finwe already knew him. "We need information about the shapeshifter," Kairos began, his voice steady despite the weight of the task ahead. "It was unleashed when the new lands were created, and we don't know where to start."

Finwe nodded slowly, his expression grave as he considered their words. "You seek to stop a creature far more dangerous than you realize," he said, his voice filled with the weight of centuries of knowledge. "The shapeshifter is no mere foe. It is an ancient being, born in the fires of the wars fought long before your time. It was sealed away for a reason. The magic of the new lands has broken its prison, and now it walks the world once more."

Otona crossed her arms, her voice tight with concern. "So, how do we stop it?"

Finwe sighed, leaning forward slightly, his eyes flickering with the wisdom of someone who had seen countless battles unfold. "There may be a way," he said slowly, as if weighing the cost of his words. "The shapeshifter thrives on chaos and instability, which is why it grows stronger in these lands. But there is a relic that can bring balance—a relic known as the Seed of Life."

Kairos exchanged a confused glance with Otona before turning back to the elven scholar. "The Seed of Life?" he asked, his brow furrowed.

Finwe nodded, his expression serious. "It is an ancient artifact, one that predates even the formation of the original realms of Mulvyon. The Seed of Life has the power to restore balance to the land, stabilizing the magic that created these new lands and weakening the chaos that fuels the shapeshifter."

Gronkar, who had remained silent until now, let out a frustrated grunt. "Of course, there's always some ancient relic we need to find. And I'm guessing it's not just sitting around here?"

Finwe smiled faintly, a glimmer of amusement passing through his eyes, but the gravity of the situation remained. "No, it is not," he said. "The Seed of Life lies far beyond the Sea of Sirens, in the Land of Centaurs. Only one centaur can grant you access to the Seed—his name is Grimbold, an ancient guardian who has watched over the Seed for many generations. However, he does not give his blessings lightly."

"The Sea of Sirens?" Otona's voice was incredulous, her eyes widening slightly. "That's a dangerous journey, even without a shapeshifter involved."

Kairos nodded in agreement. The Sea of Sirens was notorious for luring sailors to their deaths with their haunting, otherworldly songs. Crossing it was no small feat, and that was only the beginning of their quest.

Finwe's expression darkened slightly. "The journey will be perilous. You will face many trials before you even reach Grimbold. And once you do, convincing him to grant you the Seed will not be easy."

"Let me guess," Gronkar said with a huff. "He's not just going to hand it over because we ask nicely?"

Finwe shook his head. "Grimbold's will have a request, and if you can fulfill his request, he will grant you the Seed."

Kairos sat back, absorbing the enormity of what they were being asked to do. The journey ahead seemed impossible, but they had no choice. The shapeshifter was growing stronger every day, and if they didn't find a way to stop it, everything they had fought for would crumble.

"We'll go," Kairos said finally, his voice resolute. "We'll cross the Sea of Sirens, find Grimbold, and bring back the Seed of Life. We have no other choice."

Finwe nodded, though his eyes remained somber. "I wish you luck on your journey. But be warned—this quest will test you in ways you have never imagined. The balance of the world rests on your shoulders."

As Kairos, Otona, and Gronkar rose to leave, the weight of their mission settled heavily upon them. They had faced impossible odds before, but this time felt different. This time, the fate of the new lands—and all of Mulvyon—depended on their success.

After Finwe's revelation about the Seed of Life, the group steps outside the elven structure, the air heavy with tension and the enormity of their quest. The once beautiful new lands stretch out before them, their fragile existence a reminder of the magic they now must work to stabilize. Despite the uncertainty, there's a sense of quiet determination in the group.

Kairos lingers at the entrance, his mind buzzing with thoughts. How did Finwe know me? The question nags at him, but now isn't the time to dwell on it. The path ahead is too dangerous to lose focus on the task at hand.

Otona, as always, is prepared for what's to come. She stands tall, her bow slung across her back. "We've been through worse, and we've made it this far. We'll face whatever comes next."

Gronkar, though clearly aware of the dangers they're about to encounter, chuckles to break the tension. "A sea full of sirens? Sounds like a fight worth having."

Kairos looks out at the horizon, where the new lands shimmer under the afternoon light. They're more beautiful than he ever imagined, but their fragility is evident. He feels the weight of the responsibility settling on his shoulders, but his resolve hardens. They can't fail.

"We'll face whatever comes," Kairos says, his voice strong. "But we do it together."

Otona and Gronkar nod in agreement, their shared determination clear. No matter what dangers lie ahead, they will face them as a unit.

The next morning, the group rises early, their wounds having been tended to overnight by the elven healers at Finwe's request. The air is crisp, and there's a stillness in the settlement that contrasts with the weight of the journey ahead.

Otona silently checks her bow and arrows, methodically counting her supplies. Gronkar sits nearby, sharpening his Warhammer, his grin widening at the thought of the battles that await them. The excitement of facing new dangers is written all over his face, but there's an underlying tension in his movements.

Kairos, still deep in thought, takes a moment to speak privately with Finwe before they depart. "Is there anything else we should know about the Seed of Life?" Kairos asks, his voice low but urgent.

Finwe's expression turns serious, his ancient eyes gazing into Kairos'. "The Seed is powerful, but it is not a solution on its own. While it can restore balance to the lands, it cannot undo what has already been set in motion. You will still have to face the shapeshifter—and confront the darkness that has taken root in these lands. The Seed can stabilize, but it won't erase the consequences of the choices made."

Kairos nods solemnly, realizing that their quest is far more complicated than just finding the relic. The responsibility weighs on him even more now. "Thank you," he says quietly. "For everything."

Finwe inclines his head in respect. "May the winds guide you, Kairos. And may you find the strength to face what lies ahead."

With their preparations complete, the group sets off from the scholar's settlement, the towering trees and ancient runes fading behind them. Their hearts are heavy with the burden of what is to come, but their purpose is clear. The path ahead is perilous, but they are ready.

Chapter 3

The group cautiously crosses the scholar's border that separates the unstable new lands from the ancient, mystical heart of elven territory. As soon as they step over the boundary, the atmosphere shifts. The once raw, unpredictable magic that swirled in the air is replaced by something more serene yet equally potent. The landscape itself seems to breathe with life, every leaf and blade of grass imbued with a subtle, calming magic.

Kairos pauses, taking in the sight of the towering trees that line their path. Their trunks are as wide as three men standing shoulder to shoulder, their branches stretching high into the sky like the arms of an ancient protector. The leaves shimmer with a green so deep it almost glows, and the ground beneath their feet is soft, covered in a thick layer of moss. Streams of crystal-clear water wind through the forest, reflecting the light filtering through the canopy above. It is a breathtaking contrast to the wild and dangerous new lands behind them.

As they venture back into elven territory, Kairos can't help but glance at Otona. Though her face remains impassive, he senses her unease. This is her homeland, and yet there's tension in the way she moves, like a visitor in a place she no longer fully belongs. He wonders what kind of reception they'll receive from the elves, especially given the unstable magic of the newly formed lands.

The air here feels thick with history. Kairos considers how they'll approach the elven leaders. Will they be open to helping humans, or will old grudges and distrust of the other races hold sway? Especially considering Otona's mixed heritage, Kairos knows they'll need to tread carefully.

Otona's sharp eyes scan the landscape. She notices subtle signs that the border is guarded—shadows shifting in the trees, the rustling of leaves that's too deliberate to be just the wind. There's movement in the distance, silent patrols of elves keeping a close watch, but they don't stop the group. Not yet, anyway.

Gronkar, ever the practical warrior, mutters under his breath, "I don't like this. Too quiet. You'd think with all this magic in the air, they'd have come to greet us by now."

Otona responds, her voice low, "They're watching. They've seen us already, but they won't reveal themselves unless we're a threat. Just stay calm, Gronkar."

Kairos steps forward, taking the lead. His hand unconsciously tightens around the remnants of the medallion in his pocket. They have no idea how the elves will react to them—especially to the fragile magic unleashed with the new lands—but they have no choice. They need answers, and they need the elves' guidance if they're going to stop the shapeshifter.

Gronkar, always ready for a fight, chuckles darkly. "Let's hope they don't see us as a threat. I don't mind a tussle, but I don't fancy being turned into a tree."

Kairos smiles slightly despite himself. "Let's keep that as our last option."

The group continues their journey, tension growing as they walk deeper into the ancient forest. The light filtering through the leaves casts strange, shifting shadows across the ground, and there's a feeling of being watched that never quite leaves them. Though the forest is beautiful, the sense of calm is tinged with the knowledge that danger could be lurking just beyond sight.

As the group ventured deeper into the serene elven territory, the peaceful atmosphere suddenly shifted. A strange sound reached their ears—low growls, the clashing of weapons, and cries of pain. Otona froze, her hand instinctively reaching for her bow as her sharp ears caught the unmistakable sounds of a battle nearby.

"Do you hear that?" she whispered urgently.

Kairos nodded, already moving forward, his hand gripping the hilt of his dagger. Gronkar grunted, hefting his Warhammer onto his shoulder. "Sounds like trouble. Let's go."

The group rushed toward the noise, weaving through the thick trees and over uneven ground. As they broke through the underbrush, they stumbled upon a gruesome scene—a patrol of elven soldiers locked in battle with a pack of grotesque, wolflike creatures.

These beasts were horrifying to behold. They resembled wolves in shape, but their bodies were twisted and deformed. Some had extra limbs that jutted out at unnatural angles, their fur was matted and slick with corruption, and their eyes glowed with an eerie, unnatural light. Their snarls filled the air as they viciously tore into the elves, their mutated forms radiating the unstable magic of the new lands.

The elves fought valiantly, their arrows flying and swords slashing, but they were clearly outnumbered and struggling against the creatures' unnatural strength and resilience. Blood stained the grass beneath them as more elves fell under the creatures' relentless assault.

Without hesitation, Kairos, Otona, and Gronkar leaped into action. Gronkar let out a battle cry and charged into the fray, his massive Warhammer swinging with deadly force. With a single blow, he crushed the skull of one of the beasts, sending a sickening crunch echoing through the clearing.

Otona quickly notched an arrow and fired at a creature lunging toward an injured elf. Her arrow flew true, striking the beast in its glowing eye, and it collapsed to the ground with a guttural snarl. She spun around, already loosing another arrow at the next threat.

Kairos moved swiftly through the chaos, darting in and out of the creatures' reach. His daggers flashed in the dim light as he slashed at the beasts' weak points, targeting their exposed joints and underbellies. He rolled beneath the snapping jaws of one of the wolves, driving his blade deep into its neck before leaping away from another attack.

The battle was fierce, and the mutated creatures seemed almost unstoppable. Each time they landed a killing blow, the beasts' wounds would begin to regenerate, their flesh knitting back together faster than they could tear it apart. The elves were growing more desperate, their movements slowing as exhaustion set in.

"We can't keep this up!" Otona shouted as she loosed another arrow, only to watch the creature she hit stagger back to its feet. "They're healing too fast!"

Gronkar let out a frustrated roar, swinging his Warhammer with all his might, sending one of the creatures flying into a nearby tree. The impact splintered the wood, but even as the creature's broken body lay motionless for a moment, it began to twitch, the twisted magic coursing through its veins pulling it back to life.

Kairos clenched his jaw, realizing they needed to change their approach. "We have to focus our attacks together!" he called out, dodging another swipe from a creature's oversized claw. "We must cut off their heads so they can't heal!"

The group shifted tactics, working together to coordinate their strikes. Kairos distracted the creatures, darting in and out of their reach, while Otona fired arrows at their vulnerable points, and Gronkar used his immense strength to deliver crushing blows.

The battle raged on, the mutated beasts refusing to die easily, but the group's determination and skill began to turn the tide. With each coordinated strike, they cut off the heads of

the creatures stopping the regeneration. Blood and dark ichor sprayed the ground as the beasts fell one by one.

Just as the fight seemed to reach its breaking point, the largest of the creatures—a hulking, multi-limbed monstrosity—charged at them, its glowing eyes filled with rage. Gronkar met it head-on, roaring in defiance as he brought his Warhammer crashing down onto the creature's skull. The impact sent a shockwave through the clearing, and this time, the beast didn't rise.

Panting and covered in blood and dirt, the group stood victorious, though their bodies ached from the exertion. Around them, the surviving elves gathered their wounded, their faces grim but grateful.

Kairos wiped sweat from his brow, his breathing heavy. "That... was something else."

Otona nodded, still catching her breath. "Those creatures... they're mutating. Whatever magic is in these new lands, it's affected them."

Gronkar looked around at the carnage. "Good thing we got here when we did. These elves wouldn't have lasted much longer."

The group exchanged glances, realizing that the new lands had brought not just beauty, but a dangerous instability. The magic that had formed this place was twisting nature itself, creating creatures far more dangerous than anything they had faced before.

As the dust of the battle settled, the remaining elves began to tend to their wounded, casting wary glances at the group. Kairos, Otona, and Gronkar stood among the carnage, catching their breath. It wasn't long before the leader of the elven patrol, Lysander, approached them. His sharp features were set in a stern expression, but there was no denying the gratitude in his eyes.

Lysander was tall, with the elegant and imposing demeanor typical of elven warriors. His silver armor, though dented and bloodied from the battle, shimmered with the faint glow of protective runes etched into its surface. His long, dark hair was tied back, revealing sharp, calculating eyes that took in the scene with calm efficiency. When his gaze landed on Otona, however, his stern expression softened with surprise.

"Otona? It's been a long time," Lysander said, his voice tinged with a mixture of relief and wariness. "I never thought I'd see you back in these lands."

Otona nodded, her expression guarded. "I didn't expect to return either, Lysander. But circumstances have changed."

Lysander's gaze flickered to Kairos and Gronkar, his posture still tense. "I'm grateful for your help, but what brings you this deep into elven lands with... unusual company?"

Kairos, sensing the elf's suspicion, stepped forward but allowed Otona to speak first. She was familiar with the customs of these lands, and their success hinged on earning the elves' trust.

"We're here on a mission that concerns everyone in Mulvyon," Otona began, her voice calm and firm. "The shapeshifter has been released. It's a threat to all the races, and we're seeking a way to stop it before it's too late."

Lysander's face darkened. He had heard tales of the shapeshifter, a creature of chaos capable of destabilizing entire realms. But this new development seemed to weigh on him heavily. "And what do you propose to do about it?"

Otona gestured toward Kairos. "We're seeking the Seed of Life. It's the only way to restore balance to the new lands and stop the shapeshifter from feeding on the chaos. Finwe told us it lies beyond the Sea of Sirens, in the land of the centaurs."

Lysander remained silent for a moment, processing this information. His gaze shifted between Otona, Kairos, and Gronkar. "And you think you'll succeed where others have failed? The new lands are volatile. Even our patrols are struggling with the creatures that now roam the borders."

Gronkar huffed, still wiping the blood from his Warhammer. "We've handled worse. We can take care of ourselves."

Lysander's sharp eyes lingered on Gronkar for a beat before he nodded slightly. "I don't doubt your abilities, but these lands aren't the same as they once were. The creatures we fought today—they've mutated since the new lands formed. And they're becoming more aggressive."

Kairos, stepping forward, spoke earnestly. "That's why we're here. We don't have all the answers, but we're not running from this. We need to reach the Seed of Life, and we need help to get there."

Lysander studied them for another long moment before finally sighing. "The chaos is spreading faster than we anticipated. I've seen more of these mutated beasts along the borders, and it's only getting worse. I'll take you deeper into elven lands, but be warned: not all elves will welcome your presence. Many blame the new lands for the disruptions."

Otona nodded. "We expected as much. But we're not here to cause trouble. We just need to stop the shapeshifter before it's too late."

Lysander gave a curt nod and signaled to his patrol to regroup. "Very well. Follow me. I'll guide you to someone who can help you further in your journey."

As they began their trek deeper into the elven territory, the group couldn't shake the feeling that their path was growing darker. The chaos of the new lands was just beginning to unfold, and they were only scratching the surface of the dangers that lay ahead.

Following Lysander through the dense forest, the group finally reaches the elven outpost. Nestled high among the towering trees, the outpost is a marvel of elven craftsmanship, seamlessly blending with the natural surroundings. Treehouses with graceful, curved architecture are connected by delicate bridges of woven vines. Lanterns of soft, glowing light hang from the branches, casting a warm glow over the settlement as elves move silently between the structures.

Kairos, Otona, and Gronkar gaze in awe at the beauty of the place. The elves live in perfect harmony with the forest, their homes nearly invisible among the trees until you are right upon them. Birds and small creatures move freely between the treehouses, and the air is filled with the faint hum of ancient magic, maintaining the balance between nature and civilization.

But despite the serenity of the setting, there's an undercurrent of tension. Elves walk with their hands near their weapons, eyes constantly scanning the surroundings. The recent attacks by mutated creatures have clearly shaken the settlement, and it's evident that the peaceful beauty of the outpost is on the verge of being shattered.

Lysander leads them through the settlement, and though they are allowed inside, the elves watch them with a mixture of curiosity and caution. Kairos feels the weight of their stares and knows they are being judged as outsiders, strangers who have brought instability to their lands.

As they pass through, Otona walks beside Lysander, her brow furrowed with thought. "It's been a long time since I've been here. I didn't expect to come back this way," she says softly.

Lysander glances at her, his expression softening. "Things have changed, Otona. Your mother and Rhylar are no different. They still hold their views, and it may not be easy to convince them to help."

Otona's face tightens. "I never expected it to be easy. But I have no choice. If we're going to find the Seed of Life and stop the shapeshifter, I'll need to face them."

Lysander nods, his eyes reflecting understanding. "Rhylar has grown strong in his own way, but he's still as headstrong as ever. He will listen to you, though. He always did."

Otona smiles faintly at the memory of her younger half-brother, but the smile doesn't reach her eyes. "I hope you're right. I've been gone a long time, and I'm not sure where I stand with them since I've been cast out."

As they approach a clearing where they'll rest for the night, Kairos senses the personal conflict in Otona's words. He has his own reservations about venturing deeper into elven politics, but he knows they'll need all the help they can get to complete their mission. The shapeshifter is still out there, and every moment they delay brings more danger to the new lands.

That night, the group settles into the small clearing offered to them, the hum of elven magic calming the air around them. But as they rest, there is an unspoken anticipation hanging over them—tomorrow, they would meet Otona's family, and with it, face a new set of challenges.

As the night deepened, Kairos found himself restless. While Otona and Gronkar slept, Kairos sitting by the fire, his mind heavy with the weight of their mission. The stillness of the forest seemed unnatural to him, as if the very air was holding its breath. Finwe's warnings echoed in his mind, and with every step, the reality of their quest pressed harder on his shoulders.

He couldn't shake the thought that something was amiss. The shapeshifter was out there, growing stronger, manipulating the fragile magic of the new lands. They had only a vague idea of where to find the Seed of Life, and the more they delayed, the more dangerous this creature would become.

As he sat by the fire, Kairos overheard two elven scouts conversing in low voices.

"Another sighting near the eastern border," one of them whispered, his voice filled with concern. "More signs of those feral creatures, but this time, it wasn't just them. There was something else... something darker."

Kairos' heart skipped a beat, his breath quiet.

"The shapeshifter?" the other scout asked, his tone tense.

The first scout nodded grimly. "It's getting closer, twisting the magic of the new lands to its will. We've never seen anything like it before. We can't keep this hidden much longer—soon, it'll be at our borders."

Kairos felt a chill run down his spine. The shapeshifter was moving faster than they anticipated, and it was clear that the elves were just as vulnerable to its growing power as the rest of the world. He realized that waiting any longer could mean catastrophe. They had to act now, before the shapeshifter grew too strong.

The scouts parted ways, and Kairos 'mind raced with urgency. He needed to tell Otona and Gronkar what he had learned. They couldn't afford to waste any more time.

As he left the fire, he made his way back to where the group was resting, Kairos felt a renewed sense of determination. The shapeshifter's influence was spreading, and every moment they delayed brought the world closer to destruction. He would need to rally the group and convince Otona to face her family quickly—there was no room for hesitation now.

Arriving back at their makeshift camp, Kairos found Otona awake, sharpening her blades with a focused look in her eyes. Gronkar snored softly nearby, oblivious to the growing tension.

Otona glanced up as Kairos approached. "Couldn't sleep?"

He shook his head. "We need to move faster. The shapeshifter is closer than we thought. We can't afford to wait any longer."

Otona studied him for a moment before nodding. "Then tomorrow, we confront Alara and Rhylar. We'll need their help if we're going to stand a chance."

Kairos agreed, feeling the weight of urgency settle even heavier on his shoulders. Tomorrow, they would face Otona's family, and their quest would take a new turn. They could only hope it wasn't too late.

Chapter 4

The group moved in silence as Lysander led them through the dense, ancient forest toward the heart of elven territory. Otona walked ahead, her face tense with the weight of what was to come. The towering trees arched above them, their emerald leaves shimmering with elven magic. Ethereal light illuminated the pathways, casting everything in a soft glow, but it did little to calm the storm brewing inside Otona.

Ahead, the elven stronghold began to reveal itself—tall, graceful towers built into the trees, their surfaces gleaming like polished silver. Bridges, woven from enchanted vines, connected the structures, making the whole place seem like a living entity rather than a city. It was beautiful, even by elven standards, but Otona couldn't appreciate the breathtaking scene. Her mind was elsewhere.

"How are you holding up?" Kairos asked quietly, moving to her side. His voice was gentle, sensing the turmoil behind her stony exterior.

Otona hesitated, eyes fixed on the stronghold ahead. "I don't know," she admitted, her tone unusually vulnerable. "It's been years since I've been here. My mother... she's not the forgiving type. And Rhylar—he was always on her side."

Kairos nodded thoughtfully, trying to offer support without pressing too hard. He had seen Otona face countless dangers with a steady hand, but this was different. Family was a different kind of battle. "We'll face whatever happens together," he assured her. "You don't have to do this alone."

She gave a small, tight smile, but it didn't reach her eyes. "I wish I could believe that," Otona said softly, though there was a hint of gratitude in her voice. She quickened her pace, wanting to get this over with.

Behind them, Gronkar—ever oblivious to tension—grinned as he gazed at the architecture above. "Fancy place for a family reunion," he said, his voice loud enough to echo. "I've got to say, Otona, your folks sure know how to live."

Otona shot him a glance but didn't respond. Gronkar's humor, though well-meaning, felt out of place, and even he seemed to sense the weight hanging in the air.

The path ahead began to slope upwards, leading to a grand entrance made of ivory and crystal. Several elven guards stood watch at the gates, their sharp eyes taking in the group with suspicion. Otona's hand instinctively went to the hilt of her blade, not out of aggression, but comfort.

Kairos noticed her gesture and placed a reassuring hand on her shoulder. "Stay calm," he whispered. "We don't want to make things worse before they begin."

Otona let out a breath, forcing herself to relax. But her hesitation was intense, her mind racing through all the possible outcomes of the reunion ahead. Would her mother still view her as the outcast? Would Rhylar even acknowledge her, or had he, too, embraced the judgment that had led to her exile?

As they reached the gates, the guards stepped aside, clearly recognizing Lysander as one of their own. Still, their eyes lingered on the group, especially Kairos and Gronkar. Humans and Beast-men were not frequent visitors in elven lands, and the air of suspicion was unmistakable.

"You're certain this is a good idea?" Otona asked, her voice wavering for the first time. Her steps slowed, and for a moment, she looked like she might turn back.

Kairos moved closer, his gaze steady. "You said it yourself—we need their help. And no matter what happens in there, we've got your back."

Gronkar, sensing the tension between them, clapped Otona on the back with a grin. "Besides, I'd love to meet the family. Any chance I get to see a few elves squirm is a good day."

Otona huffed out a breath, half amusement, half resignation. Gronkar's attempts to lighten the mood were clumsy, but appreciated nonetheless. Still, the heavy atmosphere persisted as they approached the gates.

With a nod from Lysander, the guards stepped aside, allowing them entrance. The gates creaked open slowly, revealing the heart of the elven stronghold. As they passed through, Otona squared her shoulders, steeling herself for whatever awaited beyond.

"We'll face this," she muttered under her breath, as much to herself as to Kairos and Gronkar. "But I don't know if we'll walk out with what we need."

Kairos glanced at her, his eyes filled with understanding. "We'll face it together," he reminded her. "Whatever happens."

They crossed the threshold into the elven stronghold, where beauty and tension collided, and Otona couldn't shake the sense of dread that grew with each step. Whatever awaited inside, it was clear that the reunion with her family would not be an easy one.

As the group stepped into the elven stronghold, the cool shade of the towering trees enveloped them. The air here was different—charged with a quiet elegance that mirrored the elven architecture. Bridges stretched between the high branches, connecting the silver towers to each other, their surfaces reflecting the faint light filtering through the canopy. Everything seemed designed to merge with nature, but there was a tension in the air that broke the otherwise peaceful scene.

Otona's steps slowed as she spotted a figure emerging from one of the arched doorways. Tall, graceful, and armored in light elven leather, Rhylar stood waiting for them. His posture was rigid, his expression unreadable, but as his green eyes landed on Otona, there was a flicker of something—recognition, perhaps even warmth—before his face returned to a stern mask.

"Rhylar," Otona greeted him with a cautious nod, her voice steady but holding an edge of hesitation.

Rhylar's gaze lingered on her for a moment before he spoke. "You've come back." His voice was cool, but not entirely unfriendly. There was an underlying note of curiosity, almost as if he was surprised, she had dared to return. "After everything."

Otona crossed her arms, meeting his gaze without flinching. "I didn't come here for a family reunion. We're on a mission, and we need your help."

Rhylar's eyes flicked to Kairos and Gronkar, sizing them up quickly before returning his attention to his half-sister. "You know the law, Otona. Mother made her decision, and I'm bound by it. You're not welcome here."

Kairos exchanged a glance with Gronkar, sensing the tension between the siblings. They had known this would be difficult, but the hostility radiating from Rhylar was profound.

"I didn't ask for your welcome," Otona replied, her voice sharper now. "We need to see Alara. It's a matter of life and death, and I don't have time for pleasantries."

Rhylar's brow furrowed, a mixture of irritation and something softer—concern, perhaps. "You've been gone for years, Otona. Exiled. Do you really think Mother will listen to you now? After all you've done?"

"I didn't leave by choice," she snapped, her control slipping for the first time. "Mother cast me out because I wasn't 'pure' enough for her standards. And you—" she pointed at him accusingly, "you stood by and let it happen."

Rhylar flinched, his jaw tightening. "I didn't have a choice, Otona. You know that. Her word is law."

Otona shook her head, bitterness seeping into her tone. "There's always a choice. But that's not why I'm here. The new lands are unstable. We've unleashed something dangerous—a shapeshifter—and if we don't stop it, it will destroy not just the new lands, but everything around them. Including this place."

Rhylar's eyes narrowed as he processed her words. "A shapeshifter?" His tone was skeptical, but he didn't dismiss it entirely. "You expect me to believe that?"

"It's the truth," Kairos cut in, stepping forward. "The new lands are filled with unstable magic, and the shapeshifter is using that to grow stronger. We need the Seed of Life to restore balance, and we need your help to find it."

Rhylar's gaze shifted to Kairos, studying him for a long moment. There was a flicker of recognition, as though he could sense the weight of leadership Kairos carried, but his loyalty to Alara held strong. "Even if what you say is true, I can't go against Mother's word."

Gronkar, growing frustrated, let out a low growl. "Are all elves this stubborn? We're trying to save the world here, and you're worried about some old grudge."

Rhylar's lips twitched, almost amused by the Beast-man's bluntness, but his expression remained guarded. "It's not that simple, Beast-man. There are rules in these lands—rules that keep us safe."

"Safe?" Otona echoed, her voice dripping with disbelief. "You think your rules will protect you when the shapeshifter arrives? You think hiding behind your mother's orders will save this place when the new lands collapse? You're a fool if you believe that."

Rhylar's jaw clenched, the tension between them crackling in the air. For a long moment, they stood facing each other, their past hanging heavily between them. Kairos could see the hurt in both of them, though neither would admit it.

Finally, Rhylar sighed, the hardness in his eyes softening just a fraction. "You're asking for a lot, Otona. If I help you, I'm defying Mother, and you know what that means."

"I know," Otona said quietly, her anger fading into something more vulnerable. "But you're my brother, Rhylar. I know you. I know you don't believe in everything she does. Not anymore."

There was a long pause before Rhylar finally nodded, though reluctantly. "I'll take you to her. But don't expect her to be as forgiving as I am."

Otona's lips twisted into a half-smile. "Forgiveness was never her strong suit."

Rhylar turned on his heel, gesturing for them to follow. "Come on then. Let's get this over with."

As they followed him deeper into the stronghold, Otona exchanged a glance with Kairos. The road ahead was still uncertain, but at least they had a chance.

The grand hall inside the elven stronghold was as imposing as its ruler. Tall, intricately carved pillars lined the chamber, with glowing vines twisting gracefully around them, bathing the room in a soft, ethereal light. The ceiling arched high above, filled with magical runes that shimmered like stars in the night sky. Everything about the space was a testament to the elegance and power of the elves.

And at the center of it all sat Alara.

Otona's mother, regal and distant, reclined in her chair of carved wood and stone, her silver hair cascading over her shoulders. Her armor gleamed, adorned with the symbols of her house, intricate runes woven into the very fabric of her authority. Her piercing blue eyes settled on the group as they entered, but there was no warmth in her gaze—only cold judgment.

Rhylar stood slightly off to the side, watching the interaction with a mix of tension and unease. He had brought them here, but now it was up to Otona to face the storm that had been brewing between her and Alara for years.

The silence in the hall was suffocating until Alara's voice broke it, sharp and cutting. "You return, after all this time," she said, her eyes narrowing as they focused on Otona. "Bold of you, daughter. But then, I suppose you've never lacked for boldness—just wisdom."

Otona stood rigid, her chin raised defiantly. Kairos and Gronkar remained at her side, sensing the weight of the confrontation but knowing it was not their place to speak—at least not yet.

"I didn't come here for your approval, Mother," Otona replied, her voice steady but with an undertone of pain. "We're here because the new lands are falling apart. We need your help to stop what's coming."

Alara's expression didn't change. If anything, it grew colder. "You come to ask for help, after you shamed this family and walked away from everything? Do you think I've forgotten what you are, Otona? You defied our ways, aligned yourself with outsiders—humans, Beast-men—and you expect me to welcome you back with open arms?"

Otona clenched her fists, biting back the anger that surged within her. "You cast me out because I wasn't what you wanted. Because I wasn't the perfect elven daughter to fit your vision of purity. But the world is changing, Mother, and if we don't do something about it, everything—including your precious lands—will be destroyed."

Alara's gaze flickered for a moment, but she remained unmoved. "The problems of humans and their lands are not mine to solve. I have a duty to my people, to protect our borders and maintain the sanctity of elven life."

"It's not just the humans who are at risk!" Otona snapped, her control slipping for a moment. "The shapeshifter—an ancient creature—was released when the new lands were created. It's growing stronger, and it won't stop with just human lands. This is bigger than your borders, bigger than elven sovereignty. We need the Seed of Life to restore balance, or everything will fall into chaos."

Alara raised an eyebrow, her voice cool and condescending. "Ah, yes. The shapeshifter. A being of an age long ago. You speak of chaos, but chaos is brought about by reckless decisions—decisions like yours, Otona. Your father—Thorg—was reckless. A wild orc with no understanding of our ways, and now you carry his lack of discipline. It's what got you cast out."

The mention of Thorg cut deep. Otona's father had been a warrior, a fierce orc who had fallen in love with Alara—a love that had produced Otona. But their union had been fraught with conflict, and when Thorg died in battle, Otona had been raised under the harsh judgment of a mother who resented her orcish blood. It had been the cause of her exile.

Otona's voice trembled slightly as she replied, "This isn't about father. This is about saving everyone—elves included. Do you really think you can stay hidden behind your walls while the world burns?"

Alara's lips thinned. "I have no obligation to aid in the human struggle. Our people have endured far worse and will continue to endure, regardless of what happens in the world beyond."

Kairos, who had been silent until now, stepped forward. His tone was calm but carried the weight of everything they had faced. "With respect, Lady Alara, you're wrong. The new lands were formed from the same magic that binds everything together—magic that doesn't care about borders or races. If the balance isn't restored, your lands will suffer just as much as ours."

Alara shifted her gaze to Kairos, her eyes narrowing as she regarded him with suspicion. "And you are the one leading this... endeavor? A human thief, leading my daughter into further disgrace?"

Before Kairos could respond, Gronkar, the towering Beast-man, stepped forward, his broad form radiating frustration. His fur bristled; his eyes sharp with impatience. "Enough of this! You're too busy worrying about your pride to see the bigger picture. This isn't about your family drama or whether Otona fits into your little box of elven perfection. This is about saving all of us—elves, humans, Beast-men. If you keep hiding behind your arrogance, you'll be buried under the same rubble as everyone else."

The hall went deathly quiet. Alara's eyes flashed with fury at Gronkar's bluntness, but she didn't respond immediately. Her gaze flickered between them, taking in the weight of their words.

Finally, she spoke, her voice icier than before. "You presume much, Beast-man. But you make one valid point. The danger you speak of... it could affect us all. That much is clear."

Otona saw the shift in her mother's posture—a slight relaxation, a crack in her unyielding facade. It wasn't much, but it was enough to keep pressing.

"We don't have time to waste," Otona said, stepping forward again. "We need your support. The shapeshifter feeds on chaos, and the only thing that can stop it is the Seed of Life."

Alara remained silent for a moment, her face an unreadable mask. Finally, she sighed, though it was more of an acknowledgment of necessity than a sign of surrender. "You speak of things that cannot be ignored. And though I loathe admitting it, you may be right. The shapeshifter is not a threat that can be contained by elven borders."

She rose from her seat, her towering presence casting a long shadow over them. "Very well. I will hear you out further. But know this, Otona—I do not forgive easily, and this does not absolve you of your past. I will help for the sake of the realm, but my trust in you has long since been broken."

Otona held her mother's gaze, the weight of their fractured relationship hanging heavily in the air. "I'm not asking for your forgiveness, Mother. I'm asking for your help."

Alara gave a curt nod, her expression hard. "Then let us see if you can earn it."

The hall felt suffocating as tension simmered between Alara, Rhylar, and Otona. The grandeur of the space, with its towering pillars and shimmering vines, only made the emotional weight of the conversation more oppressive. Alara stood tall, her cold eyes sweeping over her children, but there was a crack in her perfect veneer—a subtle tremor of uncertainty that hadn't been there before.

Rhylar, with his arms crossed and jaw set, looked directly at his mother, his usual composure strained. "We can't just stand by while the world falls apart," he said, his voice sharp but controlled. "This isn't about human lands, Mother. The chaos will reach us too. You can't hide behind our walls forever."

Alara's gaze hardened. "You speak as if I don't understand the gravity of this situation, Rhylar. But I must think of our people first. The elves have remained strong by not meddling in the affairs of others. If we involve ourselves now, we risk everything we've worked to protect."

Rhylar shook his head, disbelief flashing in his eyes. "Worked to protect? Or worked to isolate? You've built these walls so high that you've blinded yourself to what's happening outside of them! You're so focused on preserving what we have that you can't see the danger closing in."

Otona stood silently between them, torn. She had long imagined what it would be like to confront her mother again, but seeing Rhylar openly challenge Alara was something she hadn't expected. Rhylar had always been the dutiful son, the one who followed their mother's orders without question. Now, for the first time, he was standing up to her, and Otona wasn't sure what to make of it.

Alara's expression darkened, her voice dropping to a cold whisper. "You dare question me? After everything I have done for this family, for our people?"

"Yes, I do," Rhylar replied, his tone unwavering. "Because for once, I see things clearly. The world is changing, and if we don't adapt, we'll be swept away by it. The shapeshifter isn't just a threat to the humans or the Beast-man—it's a threat to all of us. If we don't help now, there might not be a future for the elves to protect."

Otona glanced between them, unsure of whether to speak up. She knew the risks, understood the urgency of their quest, but there was something deeply personal in this argument. It wasn't just about the shapeshifter or the new lands—it was about family, pride, and the scars of the past.

Alara's lips tightened into a thin line. She had always been an immovable force, never one to show weakness. But Rhylar's words seemed to hit her in a way that nothing else had. For the first time in years, Otona saw a flicker of doubt cross her mother's face.

"You think I don't know what's at stake?" Alara's voice trembled slightly, though she quickly regained her composure. "I've ruled these lands for centuries. I've protected our people from countless threats. But this... this is different. If we step outside of our borders, we risk everything."

Rhylar took a step closer to his mother, his voice softening but still resolute. "We risk everything by doing nothing. The elves can't stay neutral forever, Mother. The world won't allow it."

The hall fell into a heavy silence. Alara's gaze drifted from Rhylar to Otona, her expression unreadable. For a moment, it seemed like she might lash out, but instead, she closed her eyes, exhaling slowly. When she opened them again, the steely resolve had returned, but there was a hint of something else—a crack in her armor.

"I will not be questioned in my own home," she said finally, her tone still cold but less sharp. "But... perhaps you're right, Rhylar. Perhaps we cannot stand idly by while the world around us crumbles."

Otona felt a tightness in her chest ease slightly. It wasn't a full victory, but it was something. Alara had always been so rigid, so unyielding, but for the first time, she was acknowledging the possibility of another path.

Rhylar gave a small nod, his shoulders relaxing slightly. "That's all I'm asking for, Mother. A chance to help, to protect not just the elves, but everyone."

Alara turned her back to them, walking toward the towering windows that overlooked the vast elven lands. Her voice, when it came, was barely above a whisper. "I will consider your request. But know this—I will not be swayed by emotions or familial ties. The safety of the elves will always come first."

The air remained tense, but Otona knew that this was the closest they had come to breaking through to Alara. It wasn't the end of their conflict, but it was a start. The past still loomed large between them, but for the first time, there was a glimmer of hope that they could move forward.

The tension in the grand hall finally eased, but it was far from gone. Alara stood by the tall windows, her back to the group as she stared out over the sprawling forests of the elven lands. The room, which had felt stifling with unresolved emotion moments before, now carried a faint glimmer of hope—though it was fragile, like a flickering flame that could easily be snuffed out.

Alara's voice broke the silence, calm but sharp. "I will help you," she said, turning to face them. Her eyes, though still cold, held a trace of reluctant acceptance. "But only because the shapeshifter poses a danger too great to ignore, not because I trust you or your cause."

Otona met her mother's gaze, her jaw tight but her relief evident. "That's all we ask," she said, her voice steady despite the years of unresolved bitterness between them.

Alara inclined her head slightly, a gesture of acknowledgment more than approval. "I will grant you access to our storerooms. There are supplies and a relic called The Crystal of Whispered Dreams that may assist you in your journey. But understand this—if you fail, it will not just be the humans or this Beast-man who suffer. The elves will also feel the consequences of this shapeshifter's actions. The balance of Mulvyon is at stake."

Kairos stepped forward; his tone respectful. "Thank you, Lady Alara. We won't let that happen."

Alara's gaze shifted to him, her eyes narrowing slightly as if evaluating his sincerity. "I hope you understand the gravity of what you're undertaking. The new lands you've helped create are already shifting the balance of power in ways you cannot yet comprehend. But do not mistake this for a sign that you have control over the future. That remains to be seen."

Gronkar, standing slightly apart from the group, grunted, crossing his arms. "We're not looking for control, just a way to stop this madness before it spreads."

Alara barely acknowledged his words, her focus returning to Otona. "And you, daughter," she said, her voice softer than before but still tinged with caution, "this mission may end in failure. You know that, don't you?"

Otona held her mother's gaze, the weight of their strained history hanging between them. "Yes, I know," she replied, her voice resolute. "But we don't have the luxury of inaction. Failure or not, we have to try."

There was a long pause, and for the first time, something akin to understanding passed between them. It wasn't forgiveness, nor was it reconciliation. But it was enough.

Alara nodded once, sharply. "Then go. Take what you need, and be swift. The longer the shapeshifter remains free, the more dangerous it becomes."

With that, the room fell into silence once more. The decision had been made, and while the emotional rift between Otona and her mother had not healed, there was a sense of closure. Otona had come for help, and despite the bitterness of the past, she had received it.

As the group turned to leave, Rhylar caught Otona's eye and gave her a small, almost imperceptible nod of approval. She returned it, grateful for his support, but knowing their relationship with their mother would never be simple.

Outside, Kairos, Otona, and Gronkar exchanged glances. The victory was small, but it was a victory nonetheless.

"We've got what we need," Kairos said, determination in his voice. "Now, we move forward."

Gronkar grinned, hefting his Warhammer over his shoulder. "Finally. Let's get out of this place and get to work."

Otona, quiet but resolute, fell into step beside them. They were one step closer to their goal, and with the resources from the elves, they had a better chance of succeeding. But as they left the stronghold, Otona couldn't shake the feeling that the cost of this victory had been far greater than anyone realized.

The elven stronghold receded into the distance as the group moved deeper into the forest, the towering trees growing denser around them. Sunlight filtered through the thick canopy, casting long shadows across the forest floor, making the woods seem even more ancient and foreboding. The beauty of the forest, once a source of serenity, now felt cold and distant—much like the family Otona had just confronted.

Otona led the way, her steps swift but tense, her mind clearly still wrestling with the emotions stirred by her encounter with her mother, Alara, and her half-brother, Rhylar. Though Alara had begrudgingly agreed to help, it had come with the same emotional distance that had defined their relationship since Otona's exile.

Behind her, Kairos and Gronkar exchanged quiet glances. Kairos could see the strain in Otona's shoulders, the rigid way she carried herself. He wanted to reach out, to offer support, but he knew that pushing her to talk would only make things harder. Gronkar, uncharacteristically quiet, seemed to sense this as well, his usual boisterous energy replaced with a cautious patience.

The silence between them felt heavy as they followed the path through the forest, making their way toward the boat that Alara had told them about—a small vessel docked at a river that would lead them to the Sea of Sirens. It was their only way to cross the dangerous waters, and the journey ahead loomed large in their minds.

After walking for a while, Otona slowed her pace, allowing Kairos to catch up to her. "You don't have to say anything," he said softly, his voice gentle and steady. "But I'm here if you need to."

For a long moment, Otona didn't respond, her eyes focused on the trail ahead. Then, finally, she spoke, her voice quieter than usual. "I thought I'd be more prepared for it," she admitted. "Facing her. After all these years, I thought... maybe something would change. But Alara's still the same."

Kairos nodded, keeping his pace with hers. He didn't push her to say more, letting her open up at her own pace.

"I don't know what I expected," Otona continued, her voice laced with frustration. "I thought maybe seeing me again after all this time might make her rethink things. But no. She's still cold, still wrapped up in her own pride. Rhylar... Rhylar's different, though."

Kairos glanced at her, curious. "Do you think he'll help us?"

Otona sighed, her gaze flickering with uncertainty. "He's torn. I know he wants to help, but he's loyal to our mother. He's stuck between what's right and what she expects of him. He's always been that way. It's... complicated."

Kairos didn't have much to offer in the way of family advice—his own past had never involved anything as complex as the web of loyalties Otona was tangled in—but he understood the burden she carried. "We'll make it through this," he said, his tone firm with conviction. "Whatever happens with them, we've got a bigger mission ahead of us."

Otona nodded, her expression hardening with resolve. "You're right. We have to focus. The shapeshifter is still out there, and these new lands are more dangerous than ever."

As they walked further through the forest, the path leading them toward the river where their boat awaited, Otona cast a glance back at the stronghold, her face unreadable. "Whatever happens with my family," she said quietly, "it won't stop me from finishing what we've started."

They continued in silence for a time, the weight of the past hanging between them but no longer stifling their determination. By the time they reached the banks of the river, where a sleek elven boat awaited them, the mood had shifted. The tension from the stronghold remained, but the group was focused on the journey ahead.

The boat, a small but finely crafted vessel of elven design, sat at the dock, shimmering faintly in the evening light. Otona, Kairos, and Gronkar climbed aboard, the sound of the river's gentle current the only noise breaking the quiet of the forest around them.

Chapter 5

As they set off, the river widened as it met the vast Sea of Sirens, an eerie expanse of still waters that stretched endlessly before them. The shimmering surface reflected the twilight sky, but beneath the calm exterior, there was a foreboding energy that made the group uneasy. The elven boat, small but finely crafted, felt woefully inadequate against the enormity of the sea that awaited them.

Kairos stood at the bow, staring out over the water, his hand gripping the side of the boat. The endless horizon seemed almost too peaceful, but he knew better. The air here was thick with something unnatural, something magical. He could sense it in the way the waves lapped too gently at the boat, in the silence that enveloped them.

Gronkar, standing near the boat's rudder, scoffed as he looked out over the water. "Sirens. Pah. We've faced worse," he muttered, though the tension in his shoulders betrayed his bravado. He adjusted his grip on the Warhammer at his side, his fingers tapping lightly as if to reassure himself of its weight.

Otona, seated toward the back of the boat, glanced at him sharply. "You may not take them seriously, but the sirens are real," she said, her voice firm. "Elven lore warns of their song. It can seep into your mind, make you forget who you are, what you're doing. And if you're not careful, you'll follow that song straight into the depths."

The wind carried her words across the deck, making the rest of the group quiet. Kairos finally broke his silence. "We've come too far to be careless now," he said, turning to face them. "The Sea of Sirens isn't like anything we've encountered. We've fought battles, yes, but here... it's different. We don't just have to fight—we have to resist."

Gronkar grunted, shifting his weight uncomfortably. "I can resist," he said, though the note of unease in his voice didn't go unnoticed.

Kairos watched him for a moment, then looked back out at the shimmering water. He could already feel the weight of leadership pressing harder. The decisions he made here could easily mean life or death, and the more he thought about it, the heavier that burden became. They needed to be smart. They needed to be prepared.

"The sirens' magic is subtle," Otona continued, her eyes scanning the horizon. "It's not like fighting a demon or a beast. They use your thoughts against you. They make you see what you want, hear what you desire most. And once they've got you, there's no turning back."

Kairos nodded. "That's why we stay focused. No distractions."

The boat sailed further into the open water, the river behind them now a thin line on the horizon. The sea stretched before them in all its unsettling beauty, its glassy surface reflecting the last rays of sunlight. The stillness felt wrong, as if the water itself was waiting for them to make the first mistake.

"We'll get through this," Kairos said, more to himself than anyone else. "We've made it this far. We just have to stay together."

The group fell silent again, each of them lost in their thoughts as they sailed deeper into the Sea of Sirens. The boat cut smoothly through the water, the wind at their backs, but the tension in the air was weighty. They knew the real danger had not yet begun.

As night began to fall, casting long shadows across the sea, Kairos couldn't shake the feeling that they were being watched. He tightened his grip on the side of the boat, his eyes scanning the horizon for any sign of movement. The sea remained still, but the sense of foreboding only grew stronger.

They were heading into the unknown, and they all knew that the sea held far more than just water beneath its surface.

As the boat drifted deeper into the Sea of Sirens, an unnatural stillness settled over the water. The wind, once steady and helpful, seemed to fade into a soft, eerie calm. The sea stretched endlessly in all directions, the sky above a dull gray. The group fell quiet, their nerves taut with tension, and the air felt heavier with each passing moment.

Kairos stood at the front of the boat, his eyes scanning the horizon. There was nothing but water in every direction, yet something felt off. His heart pounded in his chest as if trying to warn him of an unseen threat. He couldn't shake the feeling that they were being watched.

Suddenly, a faint, melodic whisper floated on the breeze, almost too soft to be heard. It seemed to come from nowhere and everywhere at once. Kairos froze, his muscles tightening as he listened. The sound was alluring—soft, sweet, and strangely familiar. He glanced at Otona, who had gone still, her eyes narrowing.

"Do you hear that?" she asked, her voice low.

Gronkar, who had been at the rudder, looked up, frowning. "Hear what?"

Before Otona could respond, the boat jerked slightly, as if caught by an unseen current. Gronkar tried to steer, but the boat resisted, veering off course.

"The boat's not responding!" Gronkar growled, pulling harder at the rudder. "Something's pulling us."

Kairos moved quickly to help, grabbing an oar and trying to steady their course, but it was no use. The boat seemed to be slipping out of their control, drawn further into the center of the sea. The whispers grew louder, more insistent, their haunting melody wrapping around them like a tightening noose.

Otona's eyes widened. "The sirens," she whispered, her voice tense with realization. "They're calling us."

A cold sweat broke out on Kairos' forehead as he felt the pressure in the air build. It pressed down on him, making it hard to think, hard to focus. The seductive pull of the whispers clawed at his mind, urging him to relax, to stop resisting. He shook his head, trying to clear his thoughts, but the sound was relentless.

Then, beneath the surface of the water, shadows began to move. Dark shapes, sleek and fast, swirled just below the boat, their presence unmistakable. Kairos gripped the side of the boat, his heart pounding as the realization hit him—they weren't alone.

"We need to get out of here," Kairos said, his voice hoarse with urgency.

But it was too late. The sea had them in its grip, and the sirens' song was only beginning.

The whispers were no longer faint. They filled the air, wrapping themselves around the group with an inescapable pull. The melody was hauntingly beautiful, a siren's call that penetrated deep into the mind, making it hard to focus on anything else. Gronkar, usually so strong and grounded, was the first to falter.

He stopped struggling with the rudder, his hands falling limp at his sides. His eyes glazed over as he stared into the water, the reflection of the strange, shimmering sea captivating him. His bravado faded, replaced by a distant look of confusion and longing.

"Gronkar?" Otona's voice was sharp, but the Beast-man didn't respond. He stood, moving slowly toward the edge of the boat, his steps unsteady.

Kairos, feeling the weight of the sirens' song pressing down on his mind, looked over and saw Gronkar's blank expression. Alarm shot through him. "Gronkar! Stop!" he called, but his voice barely seemed to reach through the haze.

Gronkar's massive form swayed as he peered into the water. The voices of the sirens were calling to him, pulling him closer. The sea rippled beneath the boat, and from the depths, ghostly figures began to rise—ethereal and haunting, their eyes glowing softly, their pale arms reaching up toward him. They beckoned him with open arms, their song promising peace, warmth, and an irresistible escape from the world.

"No!" Otona shouted. Gronkar moved like he was in a trance, unable to hear his companions, his gaze locked on the enchanting figures just below the surface.

Kairos scrambled to grab hold of him, but Gronkar was too quick. With a final, peaceful sigh, the Beast-man stepped over the edge of the boat and disappeared into the water.

"Gronkar!" Kairos yelled, his heart racing as he saw Gronkar's massive body sink beneath the waves, pulled deeper into the sirens' clutches.

The water closed over Gronkar, leaving only ripples behind. The sirens' song grew softer, more distant, as if they were retreating with their prize.

Otona, wide-eyed with fear, gripped her bow tightly. "We have to get him out, now!"

Kairos didn't need to be told twice. Gronkar was sinking fast, and if they didn't act quickly, the sirens would claim him forever.

The moment Gronkar disappeared beneath the waves, Kairos and Otona sprang into action. Otona was already at the bow of the boat, her hands moving swiftly as she strung her bow. Without hesitating, she fired her first arrow into the water, aiming for the ghostly figures swirling around Gronkar.

The arrows sliced through the air with deadly precision, hitting the water with a sharp thud. The sirens hissed, their haunting melody faltering for just a moment as they recoiled from the attack. Their ethereal beauty turned savage, their faces distorting in anger as they flickered beneath the surface like shadows.

"Keep them off him!" Kairos shouted; his voice rough with urgency. He didn't wait for a response, diving into the freezing water without a second thought.

The cold hit him like a thousand knives, cutting through his skin and stealing his breath. But he forced himself to keep moving, swimming furiously toward Gronkar. The Beast-man's massive body was sinking fast, pulled deeper by the sirens' grasp.

The creatures circled Gronkar, their delicate fingers brushing his arms and legs, coaxing him to sink further into their embrace. Their voices were soft, seductive. "Rest... Peace... Let go..." they whispered in his ear.

Kairos kicked harder, cutting through the water as he reached for Gronkar's arm. His fingers closed around Gronkar's wrist, gripping him tightly. "Not today," Kairos thought, determination burning through the icy water.

Above, Otona fired another arrow, narrowly missing one of the sirens as it lunged for Kairos. The arrow plunged into the water, scattering the creatures just enough to give Kairos a chance. He tugged Gronkar upward, fighting against both the weight of his friend and the pull of the sirens.

"Stay with me, Gronkar," Kairos growled through clenched teeth as he heaved Gronkar's limp form toward the surface. The sirens wailed, their sweet promises turning to venomous shrieks as they lost their grip on him.

With one final, desperate pull, Kairos broke through the surface, gasping for air. Otona leaned over the edge of the boat, her arms outstretched. "Come on!" she urged, grabbing hold of Gronkar as Kairos pushed him up.

Together, they dragged Gronkar back aboard. The sirens, now furious, circled the boat, but Otona fired one last arrow into the water, sending them retreating into the depths.

Kairos collapsed onto the deck, panting and shivering from the cold, his body trembling from exertion. Gronkar lay beside him, drenched and coughing, but alive. The sirens' song had faded, but the eerie silence of the sea remained.

"Next time... you're staying on the boat," Kairos muttered between ragged breaths.

Otona nodded, lowering her bow as the danger passed.

The group sat huddled together on the deck, the cold sea wind biting at their soaked clothes. Gronkar, still dripping wet from his near-drowning, leaned heavily against the boat's railing. He grumbled under his breath, clearly embarrassed by how the sirens had overpowered him.

"Sorry... I wasn't strong enough," Gronkar muttered, his voice low but laced with shame.

Kairos, shivering as he wrung out his tunic, glanced at his friend. "Don't apologize, Gronkar. The sirens nearly got all of us." His words were meant to reassure, but the tension in the air was undeniable.

As they sailed on, the atmosphere grew darker. The sky overhead shifted into a thick gray, and the once-calm waters became choppier, their ripples echoing the growing unease within the group. Otona, who had been inspecting the boat, suddenly froze. Her hand brushed against the rudder, which was no longer responding to their direction.

"The boat..." Otona began, her voice edged with concern. "It's damaged. We can't steer it anymore. We're drifting."

A heavy silence fell over the group. The boat rocked aimlessly, and once again, the soft whispers of the sirens filled the air. They weren't as loud as before, but their presence was enough to keep everyone on edge.

Kairos clenched his fists. Finwe's words from the elven settlement echoed in his mind: *Everything has a price.*

"We need to make an offering," Kairos said, his voice steady but tense. "Something to appease the sirens."

Then it hits him it needs to be an offering with enough magical significance to appease the sirens. He turns to Otona, who is already reaching into her satchel. From it, she pulls out a small, shimmering crystal that she took from Alara's storeroom—the Crystal of Whispered Dreams.

The artifact glows softly in the dim light, casting iridescent reflections on their faces. It is beautiful, mesmerizing, and full of elven magic, holding the dreams and desires of past elven wielders. As they gaze at the crystal, the faint melody emanating from it intertwines with the sirens' song. The connection is undeniable—this is what they want.

"We'll have to give this up," Otona says quietly, her voice tinged with regret. "The Crystal of Whispered Dreams... it's powerful, and we might need it later, but it's the only thing that might be enough to satisfy them."

"Give it to me," Kairos finally said. "It's the only way."

The air was thick with tension as Kairos held the Crystal of Whispered Dreams over the dark, rippling waters. The artifact shimmered in his hand, its glow reflecting off the surface of the sea. The whispers of the sirens grew louder, more insistent, like the pull of a powerful tide. The ethereal melody echoed all around them, a haunting harmony that tugged at the edges of their minds, demanding the crystal.

Otona stood by his side, her jaw clenched, eyes fixed on the glowing stone. She had grown up hearing tales of the Crystal of Whispered Dreams, its power of holding dreams and potential to shape those dreams into reality. And now they were about to give it away. But they all knew there was no choice.

"Do it," Gronkar grunted from the back of the boat, his voice low and rough after the sirens' spell had nearly taken his life. He knew how close they had come to losing him, and the rest of them along with him.

Kairos hesitated for a moment, feeling the weight of the decision. The sirens' song swirled around him, seductive and dangerous. His fingers twitched, reluctant to let go.

Gronkar, sitting at the back of the boat, ran his hand through his soaked hair. His usual bravado was gone, replaced by a rare moment of vulnerability. "You two... you saved me back there," he muttered. "I owe you."

Kairos, still holding the Crystal of Whispered Dreams tightly in his hand, nodded, his gaze distant. His thoughts lingered on the sirens' haunting song, their voices still echoing in his mind. He glanced at the shimmering artifact in his grip—their only remaining option to survive. "No one gets left behind," he replied softly, though his focus was already shifting to what needed to be done.

Otona kept her bow in hand, her eyes sharp as she scanned the water's surface, though the sirens were no longer visible. Her voice was low but firm. "You need to drop it now."

Kairos hesitated for only a moment before he took a deep breath, he loosened his grip on the Crystal of Whispered Dreams and let it slip into the dark, glistening waters below. The instant the crystal touched the water, the sea shimmered, and the sirens reappeared, their ghostly forms darting toward the artifact in a frenzy. Their hypnotic voices became a chorus of desire, fixated on the magic imbued in the crystal.

"They're going for it," Otona whispered, watching in awe as the sirens swarmed around the crystal, distracted by its lure.

Kairos took the opportunity. "This is our chance."

With the sirens completely captivated by the crystal, the group pushed their boat onward, silently slipping away from the cursed waters. As the distance between them and the sirens grew, the voices finally faded completely.

Gronkar exhaled in relief. "Let's hope we never hear that again."

Kairos, his eyes on the horizon, nodded. They had bought themselves time, but the road ahead was still filled with uncertainty.

"We're not safe yet," Kairos muttered as they sailed toward the Land of Centaurs, the lingering weight of their trials still pressing on them.

Chapter 6

The boat sailed through the calm waters; the once dangerous Sea of Sirens now seemingly tranquil. But the peace on the surface didn't reflect the tension still gripping the group. The encounter with the sirens had been too close for comfort, and the weight of it hung heavily over them all. The sea was calm, but the air between them was heavy with unspoken feelings.

Gronkar, the usually boisterous beast-man, sat at the bow of the boat, his massive frame slouched, staring silently into the water. His usual bravado had disappeared, replaced by a brooding silence. His hands gripped the edge of the boat tightly, his knuckles white against his weathered skin.

Otona exchanged a glance with Kairos, noticing Gronkar's discomfort. She felt a pang of sympathy for the warrior. He had fallen under the sirens' spell, almost dragging them all down with him, and she knew that it weighed on him.

Steeling herself, Otona walked over to Gronkar and crouched down beside him. Her voice was calm, but there was a firmness in her tone, one that came from years of survival in harsh conditions. "You were under their spell. It wasn't your fault."

Gronkar grunted, his gaze never leaving the water. "I was weak," he muttered. "I almost dragged all of you down with me."

Kairos approached, placing a reassuring hand on Gronkar's broad shoulder. "You weren't weak," he said, his voice steady. "The sirens are powerful creatures, and anyone could have fallen victim to their magic. We're all still here because we worked together. None of us would have made it alone."

Otona nodded, sitting down beside them. "We've faced worse, and we'll face worse still. But we do it together," she added softly.

Gronkar's shoulders slumped, and for a moment, he didn't speak. He just stared into the calm, lapping waves as if the water held the answers to his doubts. Then he let out a deep breath and turned to his companions. "Thanks, both of you. I won't let it happen again."

Kairos squeezed his shoulder, a silent affirmation of their bond. "We're all going to make it through this. We've already come too far to turn back."

The moment was heavy, yet healing. Gronkar still carried the weight of guilt, but knowing his companions didn't see him as weak brought him some relief. The tension in his body eased, and though the guilt would not disappear overnight, it no longer felt as suffocating.

The group sat in silence for a moment longer, united in their shared resilience. The bond between them had grown stronger through the trials they'd faced, and they knew that whatever awaited them on the horizon, they would face it together.

As the boat sailed further into the open sea, the skies gradually darkened. What had been a serene, almost soothing horizon, with the gentle hum of the water beneath them, quickly shifted into something far more menacing. Dark, swirling clouds began to gather on the horizon, creeping toward them like a shadow swallowing the light. The temperature dropped, and the wind, once a gentle breeze, started to howl with a growing intensity.

Kairos stood at the helm, his hands gripping the wheel tightly. His knuckles turned white as he fought to keep the boat steady. "We need to adjust course," he called out, his voice barely cutting through the wind. "The storm's heading right for us."

Otona immediately sprang into action, moving toward the sails. She tugged at the ropes, pulling them in to reduce the strain on the boat as the wind whipped through the air. Gronkar, still regaining his confidence after the incident with the sirens, rushed to help her, bracing himself against the rising wind.

"You've got to pull tighter!" Gronkar shouted over the howling wind as the boat lurched forward, the first of the storm's waves beginning to rock the vessel.

"I'm trying!" Otona snapped back, her muscles straining against the wind as she fought to secure the sails. The gusts were becoming stronger by the second, pulling against her every move. The dark clouds rolled closer, casting an ominous shadow over the once calm sea.

Kairos squinted against the driving wind and rain as the first droplets began to splatter on his face. The once peaceful sea had transformed into a churning monster. Waves, no longer gentle, began to swell, crashing against the sides of the boat with enough force to make the entire vessel creak.

The storm was growing faster than any of them could react. Within minutes, the sea was in chaos.

"Hold on!" Kairos shouted as another wave smashed against the hull, sending a spray of icy water across the deck. He fought to steer the boat, but the relentless storm battered them from every direction. The sails flapped wildly above them, and the mast groaned under the pressure.

Otona secured the last rope and staggered toward the bow, trying to get a clearer view through the rain. "It's coming in harder than we thought!" she yelled back to Kairos.

Gronkar, standing near the mainmast, tightened his grip as the boat rocked violently. His usually unshakable demeanor was now replaced with a grim look of determination. "This is bad," he muttered, almost to himself. "We won't last long if it keeps up like this."

The waves only grew more vicious. Another massive wall of water crashed into the side of the boat, nearly knocking Otona off her feet. She stumbled but managed to grab hold of the railing just in time.

Kairos sighed under his breath as he struggled to keep control. Every instinct screamed that they were heading deeper into danger. But what choice did they have? The storm had swallowed them whole, and now all they could do was ride it out.

The boat lurched again, throwing them sideways. The sky above was black as night, the sea below swirling in a tempest. The calm seas were gone, replaced by this violent force of nature, and their small boat was nothing more than a plaything to the raging storm.

"We have to keep it together!" Kairos called out; his voice hoarse from the effort. "We're not going down, not like this."

But the storm had other ideas. With each wave, the boat was rocked harder, and the storm grew fiercer. It wasn't just the sea they had to contend with—it was the storm itself that seemed intent on testing their very limits.

> The storm reached its peak, battering the boat with relentless force. The wind howled, whipping at their clothes and faces as rain lashed down in stinging sheets. The boat pitched violently with each crashing wave, throwing the group off balance. Gronkar, growling in frustration, gripped the ropes with all his might, his muscles straining against the elements. His guilt over falling victim to the sirens had simmered beneath the surface, but now it flared into something more volatile.
>
> "We shouldn't even be out here!" he roared, his voice barely cutting through the storm's fury.
>
> Otona, battling the wind beside him as she tied down the sails, snapped back with equal intensity. "And what do you suggest? We turn back? This is what we signed up for, Gronkar!"
>
> Her words struck deep, but Gronkar's frustration boiled over. He slammed his fist against the mast. "I almost drowned us all once already! Maybe you should've left me with the sirens!"

Otona spun toward him, her eyes fierce despite the storm. The wind tore at her hair, but she held her ground, fire flashing in her gaze. "Enough, Gronkar! We don't have time for your self-pity. We need to stay focused, or none of us will make it!"

Their argument sliced through the roar of the storm. Gronkar's self-blame, fueled by guilt, clashed against Otona's unrelenting pragmatism. Every word was a weapon, each cutting deeper than the last, as the storm raged around them.

Kairos, struggling to maintain control of the helm, felt the tension boiling between his companions. With the boat pitching and rolling, he knew they couldn't afford to let their emotions get the better of them. He shouted over the chaos, his voice hoarse but commanding. "Enough! None of us are without flaws!"

Both Otona and Gronkar paused, their anger momentarily dulled by Kairos' words.

"We've all made mistakes," Kairos continued, gripping the helm harder as the wind pushed back against him. "But we're still here, still fighting! We need each other if we're going to make it through this!"

The boat lurched violently, nearly throwing them off their feet. Gronkar grunted, catching himself on a rope, while Otona braced herself against the mast. The sea crashed against them with unrelenting force, as if the ocean itself were testing their resolve. Kairos held firm, his voice carrying over the storm's fury as he steered them away from the worst of the waves.

"We're not going to survive if we keep tearing each other apart!" Kairos shouted, his eyes blazing with determination. His words seemed to cut through the storm, reaching them even as the winds howled louder.

For a long moment, Gronkar and Otona exchanged tense glances, the rawness of their emotions still simmering beneath the surface. Gronkar's fists clenched, his guilt heavy on his broad shoulders. Otona, ever practical, was still wound tight with frustration, her fierce will battling against the storm just as much as against him.

But Kairos' words sank in.

The storm was merciless, and the reality of their situation left no room for blame or anger. They had to work together, or none of them would survive the journey. Slowly, Gronkar lowered his head, the tension leaving his body. Otona, though still fuming, nodded curtly, acknowledging that there were bigger battles ahead than their argument.

They weren't out of danger yet, but for now, the storm between them had passed.

As suddenly as it had begun, the storm began to die down. The angry waves that had threatened to capsize their small boat subsided, and the howling wind softened to a whisper. Now, the sea lay eerily calm, the boat bobbing gently on the quiet waters. The sky remained overcast, but the worst of the storm had passed. The group, soaked to the bone and utterly exhausted, stood in silence, letting the stillness sink in.

Gronkar was the first to break the silence. His broad shoulders slumped, and his voice was low, almost a whisper. "I'm sorry, Otona. I just... I couldn't shake it."

Otona, still catching her breath, glanced over at him, her eyes softened by the exhaustion they all shared. She shook her head; her voice calmer now than it had been during their argument. "We're all under pressure, Gronkar. But we have to keep moving. What's done is done."

Kairos released the helm, his arms heavy and stiff from steering through the storm. He stepped forward, looking out at the darkened horizon that stretched before them. The sea still felt ominous, its surface deceptively calm. His voice was steady, though the weight of their journey pressed on him like never before. "We made it through," he said, his tone serious, "but the worst may still be ahead."

The group stood together; their bodies battered but their spirits slowly recovering. Otona crossed her arms and turned toward Gronkar, her tone soft but firm. "None of us can carry this weight alone," she said, her eyes locking onto his. "We need you, Gronkar. You're not weak, and you're not a burden."

Gronkar, still visibly wrestling with the guilt of his earlier mistakes, let out a long, slow breath. His eyes, usually filled with bravado, reflected the deep conflict inside him. He nodded, though he couldn't quite meet Otona's gaze. "I'll do better," he promised, his voice rough but sincere. "For all of us."

There was a pause, a moment of shared understanding between them. Otona gave a slight nod, acknowledging his words, and Kairos stepped forward, placing a hand on Gronkar's shoulder. "We're all in this together," Kairos said quietly. "We'll get through it. But only if we trust each other."

The weight of their journey pressed down on them again, but this time, it felt more bearable. Together, they had weathered the storm—both the one in the sky and the one within themselves. The tension between them had not fully disappeared, but it had eased, replaced by a fragile understanding that would hopefully strengthen with time.

The sea was calm now, but the air still felt heavy with the knowledge that danger awaited them on the horizon. They had survived this storm.

As they turned their attention back to the sea, the group took a collective breath, readying themselves for whatever came next.

As the last remnants of the storm finally cleared, the clouds began to part, revealing a brightening sky. The eerie calm of the sea shifted into something almost serene. The group, still weary from the storm and their argument, stood at the bow of the boat, staring ahead as the horizon came into clearer view.

There, emerging from the mist, was land—vast and sprawling, with rolling green hills and towering, ancient trees. The land before them was unlike anything they had ever seen, wild and untouched by time. It was the fabled Land of the Centaurs.

Otona was the first to speak, her voice quiet but filled with awe. "We made it."

The boat gently rocked as it neared the shoreline. White sands stretched along the beach, and in the distance, they could see the silhouette of centaurs patrolling the cliffs. Their figures were proud and imposing, guardians of this ancient land.

Kairos guided the boat to a small cove nestled against the beach. The group worked in silence, securing the boat as they docked. The waves lapped gently against the hull, a stark contrast to the chaos they had faced just hours before. Once on solid ground, they took a moment to breathe, feeling the weight of the sea lift from their shoulders.

Chapter 7

The air felt different here, in the Land of the Centaurs. Every breath Kairos took seemed to hum with energy, and the ground beneath his feet pulsed with life. The trees were impossibly tall, their trunks thick and ancient, their leaves shimmering with hues of gold and green that glowed softly under the midday sun. Towering mountains loomed in the distance, their jagged peaks wrapped in mist, while lush fields of wildflowers stretched out before them.

"It's beautiful," Otona said softly, her gaze sweeping across the vast landscape. Her tone, however, was tinged with caution, and Kairos could feel the tension creeping over them all.

Gronkar grunted in agreement, but his hand remained near his weapon as they moved forward. The beauty of the land was undeniable, but it was wild—untamed in a way that set them all on edge. There was something watching them, something just out of sight.

"I don't like this," Gronkar muttered, his eyes scanning the dense forest around them. "We're not alone."

Kairos nodded in agreement; his senses sharpened. "Keep your guard up. We don't know what kind of welcome we'll get."

As they ventured deeper into the heart of the Centaurs' land, the sense of being watched grew stronger. The quiet of the forest was unnatural, as if the very land itself held its breath. Every rustle of leaves, every snap of a twig made Kairos' muscles tense, and he saw Otona's fingers twitch toward her bow more than once.

Then, without warning, they were surrounded.

A group of centaurs emerged from the trees, their powerful forms casting long shadows as they encircled the group. Each one stood tall and imposing, their upper bodies humanoid but their lower halves equine, muscles rippling beneath their sleek coats. Their armor, made of finely woven leather and gleaming silver, bore intricate designs that marked them as warriors. Bows were drawn, arrows notched, and spears leveled in their direction.

The leader stepped forward—a centaur larger than the rest, with a coat as black as night and eyes that glinted with suspicion. His name was Therion, a warrior whose reputation preceded him. He moved with a lethal grace; his spear pointed directly at Kairos.

"Outsiders," Therion's voice was deep and commanding, carrying the authority of one who did not tolerate trespassers. "You have entered sacred land without permission."

The tension in the air thickened, and Kairos raised his hands slowly, showing they meant no harm. He glanced at Otona, who met his gaze with a nod, silently acknowledging the danger they were in.

"We don't mean any disrespect," Kairos said, his voice steady but respectful. "We seek the Seed of Life."

Therion's eyes narrowed, and a flicker of recognition crossed his face, but his spear didn't lower. "The Seed of Life is not something to be taken lightly. Why should we trust you?"

Before Kairos could answer, Gronkar shifted beside him, his hand tightening on the hilt of his Warhammer. "We don't have time for this," he growled, but Otona stepped forward quickly, cutting him off with a warning glance.

She turned her attention back to Therion, her voice calm but firm. "We've come to protect both your lands and ours. There's a great danger coming—one that threatens us all."

Therion's gaze flicked between them, weighing their words. He didn't lower his spear, but his posture shifted, less aggressive and more cautious. "If you speak the truth, you'll have to prove it. Follow us, but be warned: if you attempt to deceive us, you will not leave these lands alive."

With a sharp motion, Therion signaled to his warriors, and they began to lead the group deeper into the forest.

Kairos exchanged a look with Otona and Gronkar, the weight of the centaur's warning hanging heavy in the air.

The group moved in tense silence, surrounded by the imposing centaur warriors. Each movement felt weighted, as if one wrong word or gesture would turn the situation violent. Therion, the leader of the centaur patrol, had his spear pointed at Kairos, his sharp eyes fixed on them with suspicion. The wind rustled the golden leaves overhead, but the tension between the two sides was palpable, thicker than the forest air.

"You've trespassed on sacred ground," Therion said, his voice cold and steady. "Centaurs do not take kindly to outsiders walking our lands uninvited. What makes you think you're worthy to be here?"

Gronkar, always one to speak his mind, stepped forward with a growl, gripping the hilt of his Warhammer. "We didn't come here to ask for permission. We came to find Grimbold and get the Seed of Life. We don't have time to—"

Otona shot him a sharp look, cutting him off before his bluntness could escalate the already precarious situation. She stepped forward, her tone measured and diplomatic. "Therion, we understand this is your land, and we mean no disrespect. But we didn't come here lightly. The new lands were born from dark magic, and there's a shapeshifter loose—one that threatens us all, including your people. We've come seeking the Seed of Life to stop it before it destroys everything."

Therion's spear lowered slightly, but his eyes remained hard. "Words from outsiders mean little to me. You speak of danger, but for all we know, you could be the ones bringing it here."

Kairos took a deep breath and stepped beside Otona, sensing the conversation needed a different approach. "We were there when the new lands formed," he said calmly. "The power that brought them into being was twisted. We saw the creatures that it awoke. If we don't find a way to balance the magic, it will spread, consuming everything in its path—including your lands."

The centaur warriors murmured amongst themselves, their unease growing. Therion's eyes flicked over to his warriors before returning to Kairos, Otona, and Gronkar. The skepticism in his gaze remained, but it was clear he was weighing their words.

"And you believe the Seed of Life will save us?" Therion asked, his voice sharp with doubt.

Otona nodded firmly. "It's the only hope we have. Finwe, one of the wisest of the elves, told us that Grimbold is the guardian of the Seed. We need it to restore balance, to stop the chaos from spreading."

Therion's eyes narrowed. "Grimbold does not meet with outsiders lightly. What makes you think he would grant you such a gift?"

Gronkar bristled, his frustration evident. "Because we're the only ones doing something about this! We didn't travel across seas and fight sirens just to be turned away because you don't trust us!"

Otona shot Gronkar another look, but Kairos stepped in smoothly, his voice steady. "We're willing to prove ourselves if necessary. We know how valuable the Seed is, and we respect your customs. We wouldn't ask this of you if it wasn't a matter of survival for us all."

Therion remained silent for a long moment, his eyes scanning the group as though he could measure their worth with a glance. Finally, he lowered his spear completely, though the wariness did not leave his face.

"Prove yourselves, then," Therion said, his voice low and commanding. "Centaurs do not give their trust lightly, and Grimbold will not entertain your request until he knows you are worthy. We will lead you deeper into our lands, but there is a trial you must face first. Only if you survive will we take you to Grimbold."

Otona's shoulders relaxed slightly, and she exchanged a glance with Kairos and Gronkar. The tension between them and the centaurs had not disappeared, but they had managed to avoid a direct confrontation—for now.

"Lead the way," Kairos said, his voice resolute.

Therion gave a sharp nod, his warriors following suit as they prepared to lead the group deeper into the forest.

Therion led the group deeper into the forest, where the air felt charged with an ancient energy. The trees were impossibly tall, their golden leaves shimmering in the filtered sunlight. There was a quiet reverence to the place, as if the land itself was watching their every move. They soon reached a hidden glade, encircled by towering trees and dense undergrowth. The ground beneath their feet was soft, covered in moss and fallen leaves.

"This is where you will prove yourselves," Therion announced, his voice carrying the weight of tradition. "The Drathak roams these lands. A creature born of both the earth's grace and its fury. It is your task to defeat it and prove that you are worthy of Grimbold's audience."

Otona, Kairos, and Gronkar exchanged wary glances. The name "Drathak" meant nothing to them, but they could sense the gravity of the trial ahead. Kairos, ever the leader, took a step forward. "We'll face it. Together."

Therion nodded once and gave a sharp whistle. The sound echoed through the glade, and for a moment, everything was still. Then, from the shadows of the forest, a rustling sound began, growing louder with each passing second. The air seemed to hum with anticipation.

Suddenly, the Drathak emerged. It was a massive, mutated beast—a terrifying blend of stag and predator. Its body was muscular and sleek, its fur matted with dirt and blood. Its eyes glowed with a predatory intelligence, and its antlers were jagged, sharp like spears. With a guttural snarl, the creature circled them, its powerful legs tensed, ready to strike.

"Stay focused," Kairos muttered, drawing his daggers. "We take it down together."

The Drathak moved with a speed that defied its size, lunging at Gronkar first. The beast-man roared in response, raising his Warhammer just in time to block its antlers, the force of the blow pushing him back several steps. Gronkar gritted his teeth, his muscles straining as he pushed the creature back.

"Hit it while it's distracted!" Otona shouted, already nocking an arrow in her bow. She released it, the arrow flying true and sinking into the Drathak's flank. The beast bellowed in pain, its head snapping toward her.

Kairos moved swiftly, darting around the side of the creature. His agility allowed him to slip through the underbrush unnoticed, his twin blades glinting as he aimed for the Drathak's vulnerable underbelly. He slashed at its legs, forcing the beast to stumble.

The Drathak roared in frustration, swinging its antlers in a wild arc, narrowly missing Otona as she rolled out of the way. She fired again, another arrow embedding itself into the creature's neck. "It's not going down easily!" she called, her breath quickening.

Gronkar, fueled by adrenaline, charged forward, his Warhammer raised high. "We finish it now!" he bellowed, bringing his weapon down with all his might onto the Drathak's back. The impact sent a tremor through the ground, and the creature howled in pain, its legs buckling beneath it.

Kairos seized the moment, leaping onto the Drathak's back and plunging his blades into the creature's spine. The beast gave one final, agonized roar before collapsing onto the forest floor, its massive body heaving before falling still.

For a few heart-pounding moments, the glade was silent, save for the heavy breathing of the group. They stood over the Drathak's body, their weapons bloodied, their muscles aching from the intense fight. It had been a brutal battle, but they had succeeded.

Therion stepped forward, his gaze appraising. There was no denying the respect in his eyes. "You've proven yourselves," he said, his voice even. "The Drathak is a formidable creature, and you worked together to bring it down. Grimbold will see you."

Kairos wiped the sweat from his brow, offering a slight nod to Therion. "We're ready."

Otona approached Gronkar, clapping him on the back. "Good work, Gronkar. We couldn't have done it without you."

Gronkar, still catching his breath, grinned. "I told you; I wouldn't let you down."

There was a sense of camaraderie among the group, a bond forged through shared struggle. They had faced the test and emerged victorious, and though the journey ahead was still filled with uncertainty, they felt stronger for it.

Therion gestured for them to follow. "Come. Grimbold awaits. But know this—his decision will not be made lightly."

As they prepared to leave the glade, Kairos couldn't help but glance at the fallen Drathak one last time. It had been a beast of both beauty and terror, much like the land they now walked through. But for now, they had proven they were capable.

After the group's victory over the Drathak, Therion led them through the sprawling fields and dense forests of the centaur lands. As they walked, he spoke of the centaurs' ancient traditions, their bond with the land, and their role as its protectors. The land of the centaurs was unlike any they had ever seen—untouched by the corruption that plagued other parts of Mulvyon. The trees stood tall and proud, their leaves golden in the fading light, and the air was thick with the scent of earth and wildflowers.

"We are not just warriors," Therion explained, his tone reverent. "We are the guardians of life itself. The Seed of Life is the last of the sacred relics. It is not a weapon, but a force of creation, capable of healing and restoring the land. But with that power comes responsibility."

Kairos listened intently, his eyes scanning the horizon. He felt the weight of their mission more acutely now, knowing that the Seed of Life was no simple artifact. "We need the Seed to stop the shapeshifter and stabilize the new lands," he said. "But I understand why you would protect it so fiercely."

Therion gave him a sidelong glance. "The Seed is a living part of our history. It was given to our ancestors to guard when the first wars of Mulvyon scarred the earth. Grimbold has watched over it for centuries. He will not part with it easily."

As they moved deeper into the centaur lands, the air seemed to hum with energy. Soon, they reached the heart of the territory—a secluded sanctuary nestled between towering trees. At the center of this sacred place stood Grimbold.

Grimbold was unlike any centaur they had seen. His body, though aged, radiated immense strength. His silver mane flowed freely down his back, and his eyes, dark and full of wisdom, held the weight of countless years. Around his neck hung a pendant shaped like the Seed itself, glowing faintly in the evening light.

He studied the group in silence for a moment before, his voice deep and resonant. "I know why you've come," Grimbold said, his gaze falling on each of them in turn. "You seek the Seed of Life. But before I part with it, you must understand the gravity of what you ask. The Seed is not just a relic—it is life itself. It cannot be wielded carelessly."

Kairos stepped forward, meeting Grimbold's gaze. "We don't intend to misuse it. The new lands are unstable, and the shapeshifter—if we don't stop it, everything we fought for will be lost."

Grimbold's expression didn't change, but his voice softened slightly. "I have watched over the Seed for longer than you can imagine. My people have protected it through wars, through times of peace, and through the destruction of entire kingdoms. Its power is beyond what you can comprehend. But I am not blind to the suffering of the world outside our lands."

Otona nodded in agreement. "We know the responsibility it holds. But without it, the new lands will collapse, and the darkness will spread."

Grimbold was silent for a long moment, his eyes distant as if he were gazing far beyond the present. Then he spoke, his voice carrying the weight of a decision that had taken him years to make. "I will grant you the Seed of Life. But there is something I must ask of you in return."

The group exchanged glances; tension thick in the air. "What is it?" Kairos asked cautiously.

Grimbold's gaze grew distant, as though he were lost in a memory. "I have spent my life watching over this land, never leaving, never seeing the world beyond our borders. My one request is this: take me to the new lands before I die. Let me see with my own eyes what the Seed will be used to restore."

Otona and Gronkar exchanged uneasy looks. The journey was already dangerous, and bringing an ancient centaur like Grimbold would add a layer of complexity. But there was no other way.

Kairos nodded, understanding the gravity of Grimbold's request. "We'll do it. We'll take you to the new lands."

Grimbold studied them carefully for another moment before giving a solemn nod. "Very well. Prepare yourselves. The path ahead is long, and the challenges will only grow."

The decision had been made. They would take Grimbold with them—carrying not just the Seed of Life, but the wisdom and burden of a guardian who had watched over it for centuries.

The air was heavy with tension after Grimbold's request. The ancient centaur, towering and wise, had laid down his one condition: to be taken to the new lands before his death. Kairos, Otona, and Gronkar stood in silence, exchanging uncertain glances. They all understood the gravity of what Grimbold was asking. This wasn't just about taking a powerful relic—it was about guiding one of the most revered figures in centaur history across dangerous, unforgiving terrain.

Otona broke the silence first, her voice low but steady. "Taking Grimbold with us will slow us down. We're heading back through treacherous territory, with the shapeshifter lurking and the new lands still unstable."

Kairos nodded; his brow furrowed in thought. "I know. But without the Seed of Life, none of it matters. We need it to save the new lands. To save everything."

"Not to mention," Otona added, "we've already seen what those lands can do to people, to creatures. Who knows what we'll face on the way back."

Gronkar, who had remained silent until now, stepped forward, his massive arms crossed over his chest. "And we'll be protecting him too?" His tone was sharp. "Grimbold may be strong, but he's old. If things get bad, we'll have to defend him as well as ourselves. That's more risk, more danger."

Otona met Gronkar's eyes, her expression serious. "I know. But what other choice do we have? The Seed is the only way to stabilize the new lands. Without it, they'll crumble, and the shapeshifter will thrive in that chaos."

Gronkar grumbled under his breath, his frustration clear. "I'm not saying it's the wrong choice, but it's a hard one. I'm not sure we can afford the extra burden."

Kairos took a deep breath, his gaze shifting between Otona and Gronkar. "I hear both of you, but we have to think about the bigger picture. If we fail, if the lands fall apart, everything we've fought for is gone. The Seed is our best hope."

Gronkar let out a heavy sigh, glancing over at Grimbold, who stood tall and proud a few feet away, watching them with patient eyes. "Fine," he muttered. "We take him with us. But we're going to need every bit of strength we've got if we're going to pull this off."

Kairos turned to Grimbold, walking toward the ancient centaur with resolve in his step. "We'll take you to the new lands," he said, his voice firm. "It won't be easy, but we'll get you there."

Grimbold nodded slowly, a look of quiet understanding on his face. "I thank you for your courage," he said, his voice deep and resonant. "This journey will test you all in ways you have not yet imagined. But I believe in the strength you've already shown."

With that decision made, the group gathered their belongings, steeling themselves for the journey ahead. The new lands called to them, full of danger and uncertainty. But now, they carried the hope of saving them, along with the responsibility of guiding Grimbold to his final destination.

As they set off, the weight of their decision settled over them, but there was no turning back. The next phase of their journey had begun.

Chapter 8

The sun cast long shadows over the centaur lands as the group embarked on the next leg of their journey, their small boat cutting smoothly through the clear waters. Grimbold, the ancient centaur, stood at the bow, his eyes sharp despite his age, scanning the horizon. Kairos, Otona, and Gronkar sat behind him, each lost in their own thoughts as the boat drifted toward the towering mountains in the distance, where the giants awaited.

The landscape had begun to change. The once lush and magical centaur lands gave way to rougher, more treacherous terrain. Sharp rocks jutted out from the earth, and the air was thick with the residue of wild magic—an aftereffect of the new lands' creation. The ground seemed to shift beneath them, as if the very land was alive and unstable.

Grimbold's deep voice broke the silence. "Where are the Sirens? I do not sense them in these waters."

Kairos, leaning against the boat's edge, looked up at the old centaur. "We made a trade. I gave them the Crystal of Whispered Dreams."

Grimbold raised an eyebrow. "A powerful artifact, indeed. The Sirens must have been pleased."

Otona, adjusting her bow at her side, smirked. "It must've had more than a few elven dreams in it to keep them busy. But we can't let our guard down. If anything, the magic of these new lands is only stirring up more trouble."

The boat rocked gently as the mountains ahead grew larger, casting dark shadows over the surrounding landscape. The path was becoming rougher, with jagged cliffs rising out of the water and strange, twisted trees lining the shore. Despite the peaceful surface of the water, the group felt a growing sense of unease, as though something unseen was watching them.

Gronkar, sitting with his Warhammer at the ready, grunted. "The land's changing too fast. It's unstable—feels like it could collapse under our feet at any moment."

Otona nodded, her eyes scanning the horizon. "The further we go, the worse it gets. This whole area could be crawling with creatures we've never seen before. And we still have to keep Grimbold safe."

Kairos clenched his jaw. "We'll manage. We've made it this far. But the giants are next, and they're not going to be easy. We need to be ready for anything."

Grimbold, silent for a moment, turned his gaze toward the mountains. "The giants were once protectors of balance in these lands, but they have been twisted by the chaos of the new magic. Be prepared, for they will not recognize friend from foe."

The boat drifted closer to the shore, where the towering peaks loomed ominously above them. The air grew colder, and the once-clear waters became darker, reflecting the danger that lay ahead. As they approached the shoreline, the group noticed the first signs of movement—shadows shifting between the trees, too far to be seen clearly but close enough to put them on high alert.

"We're being watched," Kairos murmured, his hand instinctively gripping the hilt of his daggers. "Gronkar, Otona—keep an eye out. We're not alone here."

The boat gently bumped against the rocky shore, and the group disembarked, their boots sinking into the soft, unstable ground. Grimbold stepped down last, his hooves making a faint clicking sound against the rocks. His presence brought a sense of calm to the group, but even the centaur seemed to feel the tension in the air.

The rugged terrain around them was harsh and unforgiving, with towering cliffs on either side and a narrow mountain pass that seemed to stretch endlessly ahead. Strange, unfamiliar plants grew along the path, their twisted roots pushing up through the ground as if feeding on the magic of the land itself. The group could hear distant echoes, the sound of rocks tumbling down the mountainside, but it was impossible to tell if it was the natural landscape or something more sinister.

Kairos', his eyes scanning the dark cliffs ahead. "This is it. Giant territory. Keep your guard up."

Otona, already on high alert, moved to the front, her sharp gaze trained on the shadows. "We'll be lucky if we get through this without drawing attention."

Gronkar snorted, hefting his Warhammer over his shoulder. "Luck? I'll take a good fight over luck any day."

Grimbold, his voice calm but firm, stepped forward. "Let us hope it does not come to that, Gronkar. The giants are not the enemies they once were, but they are unpredictable. We must tread carefully."

As they began their ascent through the narrow pass, the group felt the weight of unseen eyes following their every move. The tension was palpable, and though they moved forward with purpose, the sense of impending danger loomed over them like a dark cloud. The giants were close.

They just didn't know when—or where—the first one would strike.

The air grew thinner as the group ventured deeper into the mountain pass, the jagged cliffs towering on either side like ancient sentinels watching their every move. The path had become narrower, forcing them to walk in single file, their boots crunching over loose rocks and dirt. A chill wind swept through the pass, carrying with it an unsettling silence—broken only by the faint rumble of something distant, something massive.

Kairos, leading the group, knelt to examine the ground ahead. His hand brushed over a deep imprint in the dirt, the shape of a footprint larger than anything human. It was fresh. He glanced back at Otona and Gronkar, his eyes sharp with warning.

"They're close," he whispered. "We've definitely entered their domain."

Otona, already scanning the cliffs for signs of movement, nodded grimly. Her bow was in hand, an arrow nocked and ready. "We need to move carefully. If the giants know we're here, we don't stand a chance in a head-on fight."

Gronkar, ever the warrior, snorted as he hefted his Warhammer onto his shoulder. "Giants or no giants, we'll have to face them at some point. Sneaking around isn't going to keep them at bay forever."

Grimbold, the ancient centaur, stood behind them, his hooves steady despite the uneven terrain. His gaze followed the massive footprint that Kairos had found, his expression solemn. "The giants have lost much of their sense of peace. These lands have twisted them, made them unpredictable. If they confront us, we must not provoke them unnecessarily."

The cliffs surrounding them bore evidence of the giants' presence. Massive boulders were scattered across the landscape, some with deep gouges as though they had been hurled in anger. Trees, once tall and sturdy, lay uprooted, their trunks splintered as if they were nothing more than twigs in the hands of an immense force.

"I've seen this before," Otona said quietly, her voice tense. "It's like something drove them into a frenzy. The destruction isn't random—they're hunting."

Kairos stood, scanning the path ahead. The mountain pass seemed to stretch on endlessly, disappearing into the shadows of the cliffs. They were walking straight into the giants' territory, and the signs of danger were everywhere. He looked at Gronkar, knowing his friend's instinct to fight, but they needed to be strategic.

"We need to think this through," Kairos said. "We can't afford to attract attention. If they find us, we'll be overwhelmed."

Gronkar grunted, his hands tightening around the haft of his Warhammer. "I'm not afraid of a fight. And you know as well as I do, Kairos—if they want to hunt us, they'll find us. There's no point in hiding."

Otona's eyes flicked toward the cliffs. "He's right, but that doesn't mean we charge blindly into their path. We need to pick our battles."

Kairos glanced at Grimbold, who had remained silent, his gaze steady and wise. The centaur's presence was calming, but even he could feel the weight of the situation pressing down on them. Every decision they made now could mean the difference between life and death.

"We need to be smart," Kairos said, his voice firm. "We'll stick to the shadows where we can, avoid any obvious tracks, and keep our pace steady. If the giants show up, we fight—but only when we have no other choice."

Gronkar shrugged, though the tension in his shoulders betrayed his frustration. "Fine. But don't be surprised when we have to smash through a few giants before this is over."

The group pressed on, the towering cliffs looming ominously over them. Each step seemed to echo in the silence, the weight of the mountains pressing down like a living thing. The landscape was harsh and unforgiving, with jagged rocks and deep crevices that threatened to pull them into the earth at any moment.

Suddenly, the ground beneath their feet shuddered, a deep tremor that rippled through the pass. Otona froze, her eyes widening as she glanced at the others.

"They're coming," she whispered.

Another rumble followed, this one louder and closer, shaking the ground so violently that loose rocks tumbled down the cliffs. The air filled with the heavy sound of footsteps—footsteps so powerful that they reverberated through the stone itself. The group could feel the weight of the giants' approach before they could even see them.

Kairos drew his daggers, his eyes scanning the cliffs for any sign of the enormous figures. "Stay close," he ordered, his voice tight with tension. "And be ready."

The air was thick with suspense, the rumbling footsteps growing louder with every passing second. The giants were nearby. They just didn't know how close.

The rumbling grew louder, shaking the very stones beneath their feet. Kairos, Otona, Gronkar, and Grimbold stood frozen, the oppressive weight of the approaching giant pressing down on them like a physical force. And then it emerged—a colossal figure, towering above the cliffs, its rocky skin jagged and cracked like the mountains themselves.

The giant was terrifying. Its skin was a mass of stone and earth, deep fissures glowing faintly with molten light. It stood easily three times the height of Gronkar, its massive arms dragging a boulder behind it as casually as one might carry a pebble. The giant's eyes burned with primal rage as it locked onto the group below.

"So huge..." Otona whispered, eyes wide with a mixture of awe and fear.

Kairos didn't hesitate. "Gronkar, up front! Otona, flank it with arrows! Grimbold, we need you in this fight!"

The group snapped into action, knowing they had only moments before the giant attacked.

Gronkar charged forward, Warhammer raised, meeting the giant head-on with a roar of defiance. The ground trembled beneath his feet, but Gronkar's stride remained steady. The giant swung its massive boulder, the force of the attack enough to shatter the ground as it narrowly missed Gronkar, who rolled out of the way just in time. The sheer power of the swing sent shards of rock flying in all directions.

"I've fought bigger!" Gronkar bellowed, though even he knew that was a lie.

Otona, nimble as ever, took position on the cliff edge, drawing her bow and firing a volley of arrows at the giant's exposed joints. Her aim was true, each arrow striking the giant's rocky hide with precision, but the creature hardly flinched.

"It's like shooting at a mountain!" she shouted, her frustration growing.

Kairos, quick on his feet, darted around the battlefield, his twin daggers glinting in the dim light as he searched for an opening. The giant was slow, its movements lumbering but devastating in power. It swung its massive arms, trying to crush them, but its size made it predictable. Kairos dodged effortlessly, slashing at the giant's ankles with his daggers, but even his sharp blades barely chipped the thick stone.

"Keep it distracted!" Kairos called out, his mind racing to find a weakness.

Grimbold, though old, moved with surprising agility for a centaur of his age. He charged forward alongside Gronkar, his spear gleaming as he thrust it at the giant's leg. The sharp edge of the spear found a crack in the stone, and with a powerful twist, Grimbold forced the spear deeper into the fissure, causing the giant to roar in pain.

"That got its attention!" Grimbold shouted, his voice filled with the rough confidence of a seasoned warrior.

Gronkar seized the opportunity. With the giant momentarily distracted, he launched himself at the creature's knees, swinging his Warhammer with all his might. The blow landed with a deafening crack, splintering the stone at the joint and causing the giant to stumble.

"Now!" Gronkar roared. "Hit it where it's weak!"

Otona's sharp eyes spotted the exposed crack where Gronkar had struck. She loosed another arrow, this one sinking deep into the fissure. The giant howled, its massive body buckling as it struggled to remain upright.

Kairos saw his chance. With a burst of speed, he sprinted toward the giant, leaping onto its leg and climbing up its body with agility and precision. His daggers flashed as he scaled the creature's back, aiming for the base of its neck—one of the few places not protected by its thick, rocky hide.

The giant, in agony, swung wildly, trying to shake Kairos off, but the group's combined efforts kept it off-balance. Otona's arrows found their mark again and again, Gronkar battered its legs with relentless blows, and Grimbold's spear strikes forced it to remain defensive.

With a final push, Kairos reached the giant's neck, plunging both his daggers deep into the exposed flesh between the stone plates. The giant let out a deafening roar, its massive body shuddering as the blow struck true. Slowly, it began to topple, the weight of its own body dragging it down.

"Get clear!" Kairos shouted, leaping off the giant as it collapsed to the ground with a thunderous crash. The earth shook violently, dust and debris rising into the air as the giant's lifeless form crumbled.

The group stood panting, sweat dripping from their brows. They had done it. The giant lay defeated before them, its massive body now nothing more than a pile of stone and earth.

But their victory was short-lived. As the dust settled, the ground beneath their feet trembled once more—an all-too-familiar sound.

Otona's eyes widened as she scanned the horizon. "There's more of them."

From the shadows of the mountain pass, the heavy footsteps of more giants began to echo toward them.

The battle wasn't over yet.

The rumble of footsteps echoed ominously from the mountain pass, growing louder with each second. Kairos, Otona, Gronkar, and Grimbold barely had time to catch their breath before two more giants emerged, each one larger and more fearsome than the last. Their rocky forms towered above the landscape, their eyes burning with ancient fury as they closed in on the group.

Gronkar, still breathing heavily from the previous battle, looked up at the approaching giants with dread. "Two more of them? We barely took down one!"

Otona, her bowstring taut, shot Gronkar a sharp look. "We don't have a choice. We can't outrun them, and we certainly can't let them crush us."

Kairos, daggers in hand, surveyed the terrain. "We'll have to use the environment. There's a narrow ravine ahead—if we can lure them there, they won't be able to use their size against us as easily."

Grimbold, his spear in hand, nodded, though the weariness on his face was clear. The last battle had taken a toll on him, and his ancient body wasn't as resilient as it once was. "I can slow them down," he said, his voice rough. "But I won't be able to hold them for long."

"Do what you can," Kairos replied, his eyes scanning the path ahead. "We'll do the rest."

The group moved quickly, retreating toward the ravine as the giants lumbered after them, their massive feet sending shockwaves through the ground with every step. As they neared the entrance to the narrow gorge, Gronkar's resolve faltered.

"I don't know if I can do this again," he muttered, gripping his Warhammer with trembling hands. "That last one nearly crushed me. I... I don't know if I have the strength."

Otona stepped in front of him, her eyes blazing with determination. "You're stronger than you think, Gronkar. You've fought through worse, and we need you now more than ever. We don't have the luxury of doubt."

Kairos placed a hand on Gronkar's shoulder. "We're all tired, but we're still standing. That means we've got more fight left in us. You can do this. We can do this. Together."

Gronkar looked between them, his breath steadying. Slowly, he nodded, his grip on the Warhammer tightening with renewed purpose. "Alright. Let's end this."

As the giants closed in, the group positioned themselves at the entrance to the ravine. The towering beasts followed, their massive hands tearing at the earth as they moved, but the narrow walls of the ravine forced them to slow down, restricting their movement.

Otona loosed arrow after arrow, aiming for the cracks in their stone armor, but the giants pressed forward relentlessly, undeterred by the barrage. Gronkar, with a roar of determination, charged forward, swinging his Warhammer with all his might. The impact rang out through the ravine, causing one of the giants to stagger backward, but the other was already advancing, swinging a boulder at Gronkar with terrifying speed.

Kairos darted in from the side, his daggers flashing as he slashed at the giant's ankles, aiming for the joints where the stone was weakest. His attacks were precise, but the giant's strength was overwhelming, and every swing of its massive arms threatened to crush him.

Grimbold, his breath labored, used the terrain to their advantage. He moved nimbly despite his age, positioning himself on higher ground and using the ravine's natural outcroppings to his advantage. With calculated precision, he struck with his spear, using the force of gravity to amplify his blows. His attacks slowed the giants, but each movement visibly weakened him.

"We need to bring them down—now!" Kairos shouted, ducking under a sweeping strike from one of the giants.

Gronkar, now fully back in the fight, roared in agreement. With a powerful swing, he struck the giant at the base of its knee, the impact cracking the stone and causing the giant to stumble. As it faltered, Otona fired a perfectly aimed arrow into the exposed joint, and the giant's leg buckled.

With the first giant collapsing, the second one roared in fury, swinging wildly as it tried to reach the group. Gronkar and Kairos charged together, their combined strength and agility overwhelming the remaining giant. Gronkar's Warhammer smashed into the giant's arm, breaking it, while Kairos scaled its back, his daggers flashing as he struck at the creature's neck.

In a final coordinated effort, Grimbold, despite his exhaustion, charged forward, his spear striking true. With a powerful thrust, he drove the spear deep into the giant's chest, piercing through the stone armor. The giant let out a final, ear-splitting roar before collapsing to the ground with a thunderous crash.

Silence fell over the ravine, the echoes of the battle fading into the distance. The group stood, battered and breathless, surrounded by the fallen giants.

"We did it," Otona panted, wiping sweat and dirt from her brow.

Gronkar nodded, leaning on his Warhammer for support. "Barely."

Kairos, his chest heaving, looked over at Grimbold. The ancient centaur was clearly spent, his body trembling from exertion, but he remained standing, his spear still in hand.

"We survived," Kairos said, his voice firm but tired.

The group huddled together in a small cave, the cold wind howling outside, providing a stark contrast to the warmth of the fire crackling before them. They were battered, bruised, and utterly drained from the battle with the giants. The flickering flames cast shadows across their faces, highlighting the exhaustion in their eyes.

Kairos, still catching his breath, winced as he pressed a cloth against a cut on his arm. He glanced at the others. Gronkar sat nearby, his Warhammer leaning against the cave wall, his body slumped from fatigue. Otona was silently tending to her arrows, her gaze occasionally drifting toward Grimbold, who rested with his back against the cave wall, his breaths labored but steady.

"We barely made it through that one," Otona said, breaking the heavy silence. Her voice was quiet, but the gravity of her words hung in the air.

Gronkar grunted in agreement, his face etched with weariness. "Those giants... they nearly crushed us." He glanced over at Kairos and

Otona. "But we did it. Thanks to both of you... I would've been done for if you hadn't pulled me back."

Otona offered a small smile. "We're a team. You'd do the same for us, Gronkar. We wouldn't be here without your strength."

Kairos nodded, his eyes meeting Gronkar's. "You're stronger than you give yourself credit for. It's not about avoiding mistakes, it's about what we do after them."

Gronkar exhaled deeply, a weight visibly lifting from his shoulders. "I doubted myself after the sirens... and again before we faced those giants. But... I get it now. We don't win because we're perfect. We win because we don't give up on each other."

Grimbold stirred, the ancient centaur's-tired eyes meeting the group. He had fought valiantly beside them, but his age showed in every movement. "Your strength comes not just from battle but from your bond with one another. The land we fight for, it too depends on such bonds."

Kairos looked at the centaur, sensing a deeper connection between Grimbold and the lands they sought to protect. "You miss your people, don't you?"

Grimbold nodded slowly. "I do... but I want to see the new lands and my people will have to keep living without me for I am about to go away like the rest of the world."

Otona frowned, understanding the weight of Grimbold's words. "Then we can't afford to fail. The new lands need the Seed of Life, or everything will be lost."

Grimbold's voice was steady but full of warning. "The trials ahead will be harder than any we've faced. But together, we have a chance."

Kairos looked at his companions, the fire reflecting in his eyes. "We've come too far to stop now. We protect Grimbold. We get the Seed. And we save the new lands."

The group, though worn down by the battles and the journey so far, felt a renewed sense of purpose. The bond between them had strengthened, and with it, their determination to see this quest through to the end.

As the flames flickered and the storm outside began to subside, they knew that the hardest part of their journey was yet to come. But for now, they had survived. And that was enough.

The morning light filtered through the entrance of the cave, casting a warm glow over the weary group. The air was cold, but the atmosphere among them felt lighter after the previous night's battle and reflection. The giants were defeated, but the path ahead still held many dangers.

Kairos stood at the mouth of the cave, looking out over the vast expanse of rugged terrain that lay before them. His thoughts raced with the weight of their mission—the shapeshifter still roamed freely, and Grimbold's life was tied to the fragile balance of the new lands. Time was running out.

Otona approached, her bow slung over her shoulder. "We're far from finished, aren't we?" she asked, her tone both resigned and determined.

Kairos nodded; his gaze distant. "The giants were just one obstacle. The shapeshifter is out there, gaining strength. And we still need to secure the Seed of Life before it's too late."

Gronkar, his heavy footfalls audible as he joined them, crossed his arms. "That thing won't give up easily. It'll be waiting for us, ready to strike when we least expect it."

There was a brief pause as the group processed the dangers ahead. Despite their fatigue, they had a shared understanding that turning back wasn't an option.

Grimbold, who had been resting quietly by the fire, slowly rose to his hooves. His once formidable presence was now overshadowed by the visible toll of age and battle. His breath was labored, and his movements were slow, but his resolve was as strong as ever.

"I may not have much time left," Grimbold said, his voice filled with quiet strength. "But I will see this through. The Seed of Life must be secured. The new lands depend on it."

Otona's expression softened, and she placed a hand on Grimbold's shoulder. "We'll get you there."

Kairos turned to the others, a newfound determination settling in his chest. "We're all in this together. We've faced impossible odds before, and we'll do it again. We'll get the Seed, stop the shapeshifter, and save the new lands."

Gronkar cracked a small smile, his confidence returning. "Let's hope the shapeshifter is ready for us. Because we're not backing down."

As they packed up their gear and prepared to leave the cave, the tension from the battle with the giants began to fade. The road ahead was fraught with danger, but they had come too far to stop now. Their bond had been tested in fire and combat, and though the journey had cost them dearly, it had also made them stronger.

With the mountain pass behind them, the group stepped out into the open, the horizon stretching before them like an uncertain promise. They had no choice but to press on.

Chapter 9

The group moved through the heart of the Centaurs' land, surrounded by a vast and ancient landscape that seemed untouched by time. The trees were unlike anything they had seen before—massive, towering pillars with golden leaves that shimmered under the clear sky. The grass beneath their feet was lush and soft, and in the distance, they could see distant mountain ranges that seemed to cradle the valley in an eternal embrace.

Otona paused, eyes scanning the trees. "This place... it's not like the rest of the new lands. It feels ancient, stable."

Kairos nodded, but there was a tension in the air that made him uneasy. "It's beautiful, but something doesn't feel right. We're being watched."

Gronkar gripped his Warhammer tightly, the muscles in his arm tense. "You feel it too? There's something in the distance—moving between the trees."

The group fell silent, their senses heightened. The once serene beauty of the valley took on a different edge as shadows flickered at the corners of their vision. Every step forward felt like venturing deeper into a place that did not welcome strangers.

Grimbold, who had been mostly silent on the journey, walked ahead of them. His gaze was distant, as though lost in thought, his eyes scanning the landscape like he was searching for something long forgotten. There was a certain weariness to him, as if the weight of the years he had lived, the centuries of guarding the Seed of Life, was finally catching up to him.

"Do you know where we're headed?" Otona asked, her voice low but laced with concern.

Grimbold slowed his pace and came to a stop. His eyes, filled with the wisdom of ages, swept over the valley. "The Sanctum... it lies here, somewhere. But the entrance... I haven't been here in so long. Time has a way of clouding even the most vivid memories."

Kairos and Otona exchanged glances, the uncertainty settling in. They had come so far, yet they were still no closer to securing the Seed of Life. Gronkar, ever the optimist, tried to break the tension with a shrug.

"Well, we've faced worse. What's a little hide-and-seek in a magical valley compared to fighting giants?"

Despite his humor, the tension remained. They were deep in an unfamiliar land, with an ancient power watching over them, and the uncertainty of Grimbold's fading memory weighed heavily on them all.

They continued forward, the sense of being watched growing stronger. Something about the air shifted, as though the valley itself was alive and testing them. Grimbold slowed, his brow furrowing. "We're close," he muttered, but his voice held a note of doubt. "But the entrance... it's hidden. I can't remember exactly where."

The group exchanged wary looks, knowing that their journey into the Sanctum, and their search for the Seed of Life, was just beginning.

Hours had passed as the group wandered through the valley; each step weighed down by a growing sense of frustration. The beauty of the landscape was overshadowed by their struggle to find the hidden entrance to the Sanctum. Grimbold walked ahead, his brow furrowed as he glanced around, trying to retrace steps he hadn't taken in centuries.

"This can't be it," Otona muttered, looking around at the unremarkable patch of land they stood on. There were no obvious landmarks, no signs pointing toward an entrance—just tall grass and a few scattered boulders.

Grimbold stopped, staring at the ground beneath him. "I... I thought I would remember," he admitted, his voice heavy with the weight of his failing memory. "But time has a way of stealing details from even the clearest mind."

Gronkar sighed in frustration, running a hand over his face. "Great. So, we've come all this way, and now we can't even find the door?"

Kairos, sensing Grimbold's frustration, placed a reassuring hand on the centaur's shoulder. "We'll figure it out. You said there's a key, right?"

Grimbold nodded, pulling a worn, ancient key from around his neck. It was a beautiful artifact, made of silver and stone, with intricate runes carved into its surface that seemed to glow faintly in the sunlight. Despite its age, it felt powerful, as though it held the very essence of the land within it.

Otona studied the key with interest. "That's our answer. We just need to find the door."

But that was easier said than done. The valley's magical aura distorted their sense of direction, making the search even more challenging. The group spread out, combing the area for any sign of an entrance, their frustration building with every passing minute.

Kairos knelt by a patch of ground, running his fingers over the earth. Something about the way the grass grew here felt... different. He brushed the dirt aside and saw faint carvings etched into the stone beneath.

"Hey," Kairos called out, standing and motioning for the others. "I think I've found something."

The group gathered around him as he knelt again, tracing the markings with his fingertips. The symbols were ancient, unfamiliar to any of them, but they seemed to form a path—a series of connected runes leading further along the ground.

Grimbold's eyes widened as he saw the markings. "Yes," he whispered. "These are the markings of the old ways. This is the path."

They followed the symbols, carefully tracing the path etched into the earth. After several long minutes, they came to a stop in front of a large, overgrown boulder. At first glance, it seemed like just another rock in the landscape, but as they brushed the vines and dirt away, a stone door was revealed beneath the surface.

"This is it," Grimbold said softly, stepping forward. He held the key in his hand, his expression one of quiet reverence. "The entrance to the Sanctum."

The group stepped back as Grimbold approached the door, searching for the keyhole. It was barely visible—just a small, ancient groove in the stone, hidden by years of overgrowth. Grimbold slid the key into the lock, and with a deep, rumbling sound, the door began to shift. Stone ground against stone as the door slowly opened, revealing a dark staircase leading down into the earth.

The air grew cooler, and a faint, otherworldly light glowed from deep within the Sanctum.

Kairos glanced at the others, his heart racing. "The Seed of Life should to be down there."

Otona and Gronkar nodded, the tension between them replaced by the gravity of the moment. They had found the entrance, but now came the real test—entering the Sanctum and securing the Seed.

Grimbold, visibly tired but resolute, led the way down the staircase, his hooves echoing on the stone steps. The others followed, their nerves on edge as they descended into the unknown.

The stone staircase spiraled down into the heart of the earth, the air growing cooler and more oppressive with each step. As the group descended, a faint, eerie glow began to emanate from the walls. Intricate runes, glowing with a soft, pale light, pulsed rhythmically, as if the very stones around them were alive and breathing. The sanctum felt untouched by time, lost to the ages but brimming with ancient power.

Otona's breath caught as she took in her surroundings. The walls were covered in thick, pulsing vines, their tendrils seeming to shimmer with a life of their own. It felt like they had entered the very essence of the land itself—a place where magic and nature were intertwined in a delicate balance.

"This place..." Kairos murmured, his voice barely above a whisper. "It feels... alive."

"It is," Grimbold said, his voice heavy with reverence. "The Seed of Life is not just an artifact. It is the beating heart of the land."

As they reached the bottom of the stairs, the sanctum opened into a vast, underground chamber. The air was thick with the scent of old earth, mingled with the potent magic that filled the space. The faint glow from the runes cast dancing shadows across the walls, giving the entire chamber an ethereal quality. It felt sacred—a place meant only for those with the deepest connection to the land.

In the center of the chamber, resting on a pedestal of twisted roots and stone, was the Seed of Life. It glowed with an ethereal light, brighter than the runes that surrounded it. The Seed was larger than any of them had expected, its surface smooth and shimmering, pulsating like a heartbeat. It radiated power—raw, untamed, and beautiful.

Grimbold knelt before the Seed, his knees sinking into the soft earth. He bowed his head, whispering in the ancient language of the centaurs. His voice was low, carrying the weight of centuries of guardianship and responsibility. His prayer was one of thanks and farewell—a final acknowledgment that his duty as protector of the Seed had come to an end.

Kairos, Otona, and Gronkar watched in awe. The Seed's glow reflected in their eyes, its presence both comforting and unnerving. They could feel its power radiating through the room, touching everything around it.

"This is it," Otona whispered. "This is what we've been searching for."

Gronkar, ever practical, gripped his Warhammer tightly. "Let's not get too comfortable. If this thing is as important as it looks, we're not going to be the only ones after it."

Kairos nodded, his gaze never leaving the Seed. He could feel a deep sense of responsibility settling over him. They had come so far, faced so many dangers, and now, they were standing before the one thing that could save the new lands. But there was an unease in the air, a quiet tension that made him feel like they weren't alone.

Grimbold rose slowly, his old bones creaking with the movement. He turned to the group, his face lined with both sadness and resolve. "The Seed must be taken. It is the key to restoring balance to the new lands. But once it is removed from its resting place, we may face challenges greater than anything we've seen so far."

Kairos stepped forward, feeling the weight of Grimbold's words. The Seed of Life was everything they had fought for—but he knew instinctively that taking it wouldn't be simple. There would be consequences.

With a deep breath, he turned to Otona and Gronkar. "Are we ready for this?"

Otona nodded, her eyes never leaving the Seed. "We've come too far to turn back now."

Gronkar grunted, his grip on his weapon tightening. "Let's get this over with."

Kairos stepped toward the pedestal, the glow of the Seed growing brighter as he approached. His heart pounded in his chest as he reached out, his hand hovering over the Seed's surface. The moment his fingers brushed the Seed, the ground beneath them trembled.

"Something's coming," Otona warned, her voice tense.

The atmosphere in the sanctum shifted, the air growing colder. The once comforting glow of the runes dimmed, casting the room in shadows.

As soon as Kairos' hand touched the Seed of Life, the ground beneath them rumbled ominously. The runes lining the walls flickered as if the magic sustaining them was struggling under a new weight. Before the group could fully grasp the magnitude of the Seed's power, the shadows in the sanctum deepened, twisting unnaturally.

A low, sinister voice echoed through the chamber, sending chills down their spines. "You've come so far, but you won't leave with that Seed."

From the darkness, a figure emerged—a perfect mirror image of Kairos, his face twisted in a mocking grin. The group froze, realizing instantly what they were facing.

"The shapeshifter," Otona hissed, drawing her bow.

The creature's form flickered, morphing seamlessly from Kairos into Gronkar, then into Otona, and finally into Grimbold. It moved with an eerie fluidity; each transformation more unsettling than the last. It wasn't just imitating their appearance—it was mimicking their movements, their voices, their very essence.

"I know your fears. I know your doubts," the shapeshifter said, its voice an unnerving mix of all their tones. "You think you've come to save the lands, but you've only brought them closer to ruin."

Kairos' mind raced. The shapeshifter's goal was clear—it wanted the Seed for itself, to corrupt its power and destroy the balance they had fought so hard to protect.

"Don't listen to it!" Kairos shouted, gripping his daggers. "It's trying to divide us."

The shapeshifter, now in the form of Gronkar, grinned wickedly. "Divide you? You're already divided. Isn't that right, Gronkar? Always failing, always needing to be saved. Why are you even here? You know you're just slowing them down."

Gronkar growled, his hands tightening around the hilt of his Warhammer. The shapeshifter shifted again, this time into a distorted version of Kairos. "And you, Kairos... So eager to lead, but do you even know where you're going? Do you trust yourself to make the right decisions?"

Kairos' heart pounded. The shapeshifter was trying to get inside their heads, to exploit their insecurities. He had to stay focused, or they would all fall apart.

But the shapeshifter's eyes suddenly gleamed as it shifted into Otona's form, a cruel smile curving across her mirrored lips. "And then there's you, Otona. The outcast. The freak." Its voice was venomous, echoing with the weight of Otona's past. "Cast out by your own people. Rejected by your family. You don't belong anywhere, do you? Not with the elves, not with the orcs, and not even with this... human and beast-man."

Otona's grip on her bow tightened, her face hardening. "You know nothing about me," she spat, though the pain behind her eyes was unmistakable.

"Oh, but I do," the shapeshifter purred, stepping closer in Otona's form. "You pretend not to care, but it eats at you every day. You've been alone your whole life, Otona. Your own mother rejected you. Your people view you as nothing more than a stain on their bloodline. Do you think these fools are any different? Do you really think they trust you?"

Otona's heart raced, but she refused to show weakness. She loosed an arrow, her aim true, but the shapeshifter dodged easily, laughing as it shifted back into Gronkar's form.

"We're a team," Otona shot back, her voice firm. "I don't need to prove myself to anyone."

But the shapeshifter wasn't done. "And yet, you still crave their acceptance. The respect of a mother who banished you. The loyalty of a half-brother who never stood by your side. They'll never see you as one of them, Otona. You're just an outsider, wandering between worlds, never finding a home."

Kairos glanced at Otona, seeing the flicker of pain in her eyes, but there was no time to comfort her now. The sanctum shook violently as the shapeshifter's magic clashed with the ancient power of the Seed. Cracks began to form in the stone walls, and the ceiling trembled as if the sanctum itself was on the verge of collapse.

"You're weak!" the shapeshifter, now in Grimbold's form, taunted as it lunged at Kairos. "You can't protect them!"

Kairos barely dodged the attack, but the words struck deep. For a brief moment, doubt flickered in his mind. Could he lead them through this? Could he protect the Seed and the new lands?

"Don't listen!" Grimbold's voice rang out, cutting through the chaos. "It thrives on your fear. Stand strong!"

The shapeshifter twisted into Otona's form again, a dark smile on its lips. "You think you can defeat me? You think you can save this land?"

"We've faced worse than you!" Otona shouted, her arrows flying true this time, grazing the shapeshifter's shoulder. It snarled, its form flickering and distorting as it recoiled.

Despite their efforts, the creature was relentless. Its mimicry allowed it to exploit their every move, and the sanctum was beginning to crumble around them. Kairos could feel time slipping away—if they didn't end this soon, they would all be buried beneath the ruins.

Breathing hard, Kairos caught Gronkar's eye. "We need to trap it—corner it somehow."

Gronkar nodded, his resolve hardening. "I'll force it back. You two, find a way to pin it down."

Kairos and Otona moved into position as Gronkar charged the shapeshifter head-on. The beast snarled, but Gronkar didn't back down. With a mighty swing of his Warhammer, he drove the shapeshifter toward the center of the sanctum, forcing it back toward the pedestal where the Seed glowed brightly.

"Now!" Kairos shouted.

Otona's arrows and Kairos' daggers struck in unison, the force of their combined attack driving the shapeshifter into a corner. It hissed, its form writhing as it struggled to maintain its shape.

For a moment, it looked as though they had the upper hand. The shapeshifter, cornered and weakened, began to lose its form, flickering between different identities. But Kairos knew better than to relax. They had come close to victory, but there was still one final blow to be struck—and he wasn't sure if they could deliver it before the sanctum collapsed.

The shapeshifter writhed in the corner of the sanctum, flickering between forms—Otona, Kairos, Gronkar, and Grimbold—its dark magic rippling through the air. The group had it pinned, but they were weakening, the constant shifting of the creature's form wearing down their resolve. The ancient sanctum trembled with each clash of power, cracks forming in the stone walls as the structure strained to contain the battle.

"We can't keep this up," Otona gasped, pulling another arrow from her quiver, her hands shaking from the intensity of the fight. "It's too strong."

Kairos, his daggers slick with the creature's shadowy essence, nodded grimly. "We need to end this—now."

But even as they pressed their attack, the shapeshifter fought back with renewed fury. Its voice was a cacophony of taunts and sneers, mocking their every move. "You think you've won? You're nothing—lost souls grasping at the edge of a dying world."

Suddenly, Grimbold's voice, firm and resolute, cut through the chaos. "Enough."

The centaur warrior, his old frame battered and bruised, stepped forward. There was a new fire in his eyes, a clarity that hadn't been there before. He knew what needed to be done.

"No, Grimbold, you can't—" Kairos began, but Grimbold silenced him with a look.

"This is my duty," Grimbold said quietly. "I have served as guardian of the Seed for centuries. It was always meant to be this way. I will hold the creature."

Before anyone could stop him, Grimbold surged forward with a speed and strength that defied his years. His powerful legs pinning the shapeshifter down with a force that left the creature struggling in vain. Grimbold's muscles strained, his old bones creaking under the weight of his final act of courage.

"Now!" Grimbold roared, his voice echoing through the sanctum.

Kairos, Otona, and Gronkar didn't hesitate. They leaped forward, striking as one—Kairos' daggers flashed through the air, Otona's arrows flew true, and Gronkar's Warhammer crashed down with earth-shattering force. Their combined assault struck the shapeshifter with deadly precision.

The creature let out a bone-chilling scream, its form destabilizing as it struggled to hold itself together. The air around them crackled with dark energy as the shapeshifter's body dissolved into a swirling cloud of shadow, writhing and twisting as it was pulled into the void. For a moment, the sanctum was filled with a terrible silence as the last traces of the creature vanished.

And then, it was over.

The group stood frozen, staring at the empty space where the shapeshifter had been. For a heartbeat, it seemed as though they had won.

But the victory was far from sweet. Grimbold, still standing tall despite his pain, began to collapse, his body giving way under the strain of the battle. Kairos and Gronkar rushed forward to catch him, lowering the centaur gently to the ground.

"Grimbold, no," Otona whispered, kneeling beside him.

Grimbold's breaths were shallow, each one a struggle. His eyes, however, were peaceful. "It was... always my fate," he said softly, his voice barely a whisper now. "The Seed of Life... must be protected. You... must finish this."

Kairos held Grimbold's hand, his chest tight with emotion. "We will. I swear it."

The Seed of Life still glowed faintly on its pedestal, untouched by the violence around it. Grimbold turned his gaze to it one last time, a small smile forming on his lips. "Restore the lands... bring balance... honor my memory..."

With those final words, Grimbold's eyes fluttered shut, and his body stilled. The great warrior who had guarded the Seed for so long had given his life to protect it, and the weight of his sacrifice settled heavily on the group.

They sat in silence, grief mingling with relief. The shapeshifter was gone—defeated, or so it seemed. But even as the creature dissolved, a lingering unease filled the air. The sanctum was still, but there was an emptiness to the victory, a hollow feeling that none of them could shake.

Otona stood first, wiping a tear from her cheek. "He gave everything for this," she said quietly. "We can't let his sacrifice be in vain."

Kairos nodded, though his mind was troubled. Something about the shapeshifter's defeat felt incomplete, as if the darkness hadn't truly been vanquished, only pushed back for a time. The creature's taunts still echoed in his ears, and he couldn't shake the feeling that this battle wasn't truly over.

But there was no time to dwell on it now. Grimbold's body lay still, his task complete, and the Seed of Life now in their hands. Kairos, Otona, and Gronkar stood together, the weight of their journey ahead heavy on their shoulders.

"Let's go," Kairos said, his voice steady but filled with resolve. "We have a world to save."

The sanctum was eerily quiet after the battle. Shadows still lingered in the corners, but the immediate threat had passed. Kairos, Otona, and Gronkar stood around Grimbold's fallen form, their hearts heavy with the weight of his sacrifice. The Seed of Life, glowing softly on its pedestal, seemed to pulse in time with the last echoes of Grimbold's final breaths, a reminder of the price that had been paid to protect it.

Kairos knelt beside Grimbold, his hand resting on the centaur's now-still form. Grimbold had been a warrior until the end, his strength and determination driving them forward when they needed it most. Now, they were left without his guidance.

"We've lost too much," Otona whispered, her voice thick with grief. Her eyes lingered on the Seed, knowing its importance, but unable to shake the sadness that clung to her.

Gronkar, his usual bravado replaced with quiet respect, stood silently beside them. He didn't speak, but the tension in his posture spoke volumes. For all his strength, he had not been able to stop the inevitable.

Kairos stood, his fingers brushing over the Seed as he took it from its pedestal. It was small, light in his hands, yet it felt as though it carried the weight of the entire world. Grimbold had entrusted them with this—this was their only hope to restore balance to the lands and stop the shapeshifter's corruption from spreading any further.

"Grimbold gave his life for this," Kairos said quietly, his voice steadier than he felt. "We can't let that be for nothing. The new lands, everything we've fought for, it's all riding on us now."

Otona nodded, her eyes still reflecting the pain of their losses but filled with renewed resolve. "We carry his memory with us. We carry this Seed to the new lands, and we do what he couldn't finish."

Gronkar's fist tightened around his Warhammer, his eyes focused on the path ahead. "And we'll crush anyone who stands in our way."

The three of them stood in silence for a moment longer, letting the weight of the moment sink in. The shapeshifter might have been defeated here, but Kairos couldn't shake the feeling that it wasn't truly gone. The shadows felt too thick, the air too heavy. The real battle still lay ahead of them—perhaps one even more dangerous than what they had just faced.

Kairos turned toward the exit; the Seed clutched tightly in his hand. "We need to move. The longer we stay, the more vulnerable we are. We have to get this Seed to the new lands."

As they made their way out of the sanctum, leaving behind the memory of how Grimbold had spent centuries guarding the Seed, the group's steps were heavier, but their resolve was unshaken. They had faced giants, sirens, and the shapeshifter itself, and still, they moved forward. Grimbold's sacrifice would not be in vain.

The path ahead was uncertain, but they were ready. Together, they would carry the Seed of Life forward, no matter what dangers awaited them in the new lands. The fate of Mulvyon now rested in their hands.

Chapter 10

The group descended from the Sacred Valley in silence, the once-vibrant glow of victory muted by the loss of Grimbold. His sacrifice weighed heavily on their hearts, each step feeling heavier than the last. As the sun dipped behind the towering trees, casting long shadows on the path ahead, the Seed of Life, now safely in Kairos' hands, pulsed with a faint, ethereal glow.

Otona walked at the front of the group, her eyes scanning the landscape, but her thoughts clearly distant. Gronkar trailed behind, his usual boldness replaced by quiet contemplation. They had won a small victory, but it had come at a steep cost.

"We'll have to move faster," Kairos murmured, breaking the silence. He hadn't been able to shake the gnawing feeling that something wasn't right. He glanced down at the Seed, its glow pulsing in a rhythm that matched his growing sense of unease.

Otona, though silent, shared his concern. Her gaze, usually sharp and focused, had flickered with doubt since they left the valley. "It feels wrong," she finally said, her voice low. "Grimbold is gone, but I feel like the Shapeshifter is still out there watching."

Gronkar, always the skeptic, grunted in agreement. "Maybe that's just the land mourning him... or maybe we aren't alone out here."

The air around them seemed to tighten, the serene landscape losing its beauty as the trees loomed taller, darker. The calm had become deceptive, every rustle of leaves now suspicious. Even the birds seemed to have quieted, as if sensing the danger lurking somewhere beyond sight.

Kairos glanced at the horizon. The sky, now tinged with deep oranges and purples, painted a breathtaking picture, but a shadow loomed far in the distance, moving too quickly to be natural. It flitted across the edge of the forest, vanishing as quickly as it appeared, but it was enough to send a cold chill down his spine.

"Something's coming," he whispered, tightening his grip on the Seed.

Otona nodded. "We need to stay alert."

The group moved cautiously through the valley; their senses heightened after the unsettling feeling of being watched. The trees were dense, the golden light filtering through the leaves giving an illusion of serenity. But as they approached a narrow stretch of the path, a figure emerged from the shadows ahead—Lethiriel.

She stood in the middle of the trail, her arms crossed, her bow slung casually over her shoulder. Her cold, confident smile was unnerving. Around her, mercenaries—elite warriors, their faces grim—began to step out from the cover of the trees, flanking her. The path was blocked.

"Well, well," Lethiriel began, her voice smooth and mocking. "I didn't think you'd get this far, but here you are." She took a slow step forward, her eyes locking onto the Seed of Life glowing faintly in Kairos' grip. "You're carrying something that doesn't belong to you."

Kairos immediately stepped in front of Otona and Gronkar, his fingers tightening around the Seed. "What are you doing here, Lethiriel?" he asked, his voice steady but laced with suspicion. "You've been following us."

Lethiriel's smirk widened. "Of course. I've known every step you've taken since the Centaur lands. Did you really think you could slip past me? I've been patient, but now..." She gestured to the Seed. "Now I can't let you continue."

Gronkar growled low in his throat, already reaching for his weapon. "If you think we're handing this over to you, you've got another thing coming."

Lethiriel raised a hand, and her mercenaries shifted, weapons at the ready. "Oh, Gronkar, always so eager for a fight." Her eyes flicked to Otona, her gaze sharp and calculating. "And you, outcast. Still clinging to this lost cause?"

Otona stiffened at the word, but kept her bow steady, not rising to the taunt. "You don't know what you're doing, Lethiriel. The Seed doesn't belong to you."

"Doesn't it?" Lethiriel stepped closer, her confidence radiating from her like a tangible force. "I know more about that Seed than you can imagine. It holds the power to reshape the new lands, to stabilize what's been broken. You and your little band are in over your heads. Give me the Seed, and I'll make sure it's used properly."

Kairos frowned, sensing something more behind her words. "What do you really want, Lethiriel? Why are you so interested in the Seed?"

Lethiriel's smile faltered for a moment, a flash of something darker passing over her features. "Let's just say I have a personal stake in this. The shapeshifter is not your problem. It's mine. You'll only fail trying to stop it. Hand over the Seed, and I'll take care of it. I'll use it the way it was meant to be used."

Kairos shook his head. "You don't get to decide that."

She laughed softly, though her eyes never lost their edge. "You're wrong, Kairos. I already have decided." Her tone shifted, losing its playful edge. "I'll give you one chance. Hand over the Seed, and I'll let you walk away. Refuse, and I'll take it by force."

The mercenaries stepped forward, tightening the circle around the group. Otona's hand was already on her bowstring, and Gronkar's muscles tensed, ready to fight. Kairos could feel the weight of the Seed in his hand, pulsing with life. This wasn't just about power—it was about who controlled the future of the new lands.

Kairos' voice was calm, but firm. "We're not giving it to you."

Lethiriel's smile disappeared, her eyes cold and calculating. "So be it."

The tension between the two groups finally snapped. In an instant, Lethiriel's hand shot up, signaling her mercenaries to attack. Steel clashed, arrows flew, and the valley erupted into chaos.

Kairos barely had time to react as Lethiriel rushed toward him, her speed and precision far beyond anything he'd expected. She swung her sword in a deadly arc, forcing him to backpedal and block with his daggers. Her strikes were fast and relentless, driving him further away from the others.

"You're out of your league, Kairos," Lethiriel taunted between strikes. Her blade moved like lightning; each blow expertly aimed to weaken his defenses. "You think you can lead this little group? You think you can protect the Seed?"

Kairos gritted his teeth, struggling to parry her rapid attacks. "I don't need your approval," he spat back, dodging another swing. "We're doing this without you."

"Without me? You'll fail. You're already failing." Lethiriel's voice was sharp, her words designed to sting. She spun gracefully, her sword barely missing his chest as he leaped back. "I've been fighting since the streets of Duskreach. You? You're a thief, playing at being a hero."

Meanwhile, Gronkar roared as he swung his Warhammer, fending off two of Lethiriel's mercenaries. One soldier came at him with a spear, but Gronkar's brute strength shattered the weapon with a single strike. Another tried to flank him, but Gronkar, moving faster than expected for someone his size, turned and slammed his hammer into the ground, sending his enemies stumbling back.

Otona, perched on a slight ridge, fired arrows with deadly accuracy, covering both Kairos and Gronkar. Each shot found its mark, slowing down the advancing mercenaries. "We can't let them surround us!" she called out, nocking another arrow. Her eyes were sharp, calculating the angles with precision, but she couldn't help glancing toward Kairos and Lethiriel, her concern growing as the duel intensified.

Lethiriel's strikes were more than just aggressive—they were precise, calculated, and aimed to break Kairos both physically and mentally. She feigned a slash toward his shoulder, but as he moved to block, she spun, slamming the hilt of her sword into his stomach. Kairos gasped; the wind knocked out of him as he staggered backward.

"You're not strong enough for this, Kairos," she sneered. "You can't defeat the shapeshifter without me. You'll lose everything if you don't give me the Seed." She lunged again, her sword barely missing his side as he twisted away.

Kairos' mind raced. Lethiriel was better than him, faster and more experienced. Every move he made seemed to play into her hands. But the thought of handing over the Seed—of letting her shape the new lands to her will—was unthinkable.

In the chaos of the battle, the Seed of Life was knocked loose from Kairos' pack. It rolled across the ground, its soft glow catching Lethiriel's eye. She darted toward it, her face lighting up with victory. "It's mine!" she shouted, reaching for the Seed.

"No!" Kairos lunged forward, using every ounce of his strength to block her. He slammed his dagger into the ground between her and the Seed, cutting her off just as her fingers brushed the glowing artifact.

Lethiriel snarled in frustration, her sword clashing against Kairos' dagger as they struggled for control. "You don't know what you're doing! I'm the only one who can stop the shapeshifter, Kairos! You'll get yourself and everyone else killed!"

Kairos met her eyes, the weight of her words heavy on his mind. But deep down, he knew the truth. "You're wrong," he said, his voice steady despite the chaos around them. "We don't need you. We'll protect the Seed and stop the shapeshifter ourselves."

With a surge of strength, Kairos pushed her back, reclaiming the Seed. Lethiriel staggered but quickly recovered, her eyes flashing with anger. The mercenaries, sensing their leader's fury, redoubled their efforts against Otona and Gronkar, but the group held strong.

The battle raged on, but the tides were shifting. Lethiriel, despite her skill, realized she wasn't going to win this easily. Kairos, Otona, and Gronkar were a stronger unit than she'd expected. The Seed was slipping out of her grasp.

The dust had barely settled from the battle, but the group's breaths were still ragged, their hearts still racing. Kairos sheathed his daggers, glancing at the spot where Lethiriel had vanished with her mercenaries. Her words lingered in his mind, weaving doubt into his thoughts like poison. They had managed to hold onto the Seed of Life, but her retreat felt more like a calculated move than a true defeat.

Gronkar kicked at the dirt, still angry. "She just walked away," he growled, fists clenched at his sides. "We had her! Why didn't we finish it?"

Otona, standing nearby with her bow still in hand, stared off into the distance, her face thoughtful. "Because she didn't need to fight anymore," she murmured. "She's planning something bigger. This was just a test."

Kairos didn't respond immediately. His grip on the Seed of Life tightened as he stared at the faint glow emanating from it. Grimbold had entrusted them with this, and they'd nearly lost it. He could still feel Lethiriel's mocking voice echoing in his ears: *"You're not ready for what's coming."*

"Do you think she's right?" Kairos finally asked, his voice low, almost uncertain. "About the shapeshifter... and us?"

Gronkar looked at him, confused. "What are you talking about?"

"She said we're not ready," Kairos said, looking down at the Seed. "What if she's right? We barely managed to protect this, and we know next to nothing about the shapeshifter. How can we fight something when we don't even understand its power?"

Otona turned to him, her expression softening. "We've come this far, Kairos. Lethiriel is trying to get inside your head. She wants you to doubt yourself, to question everything we're doing. Don't give her that power."

Kairos wanted to believe her, but Lethiriel's words had struck a nerve. Every choice he had made weighed on him, and the burden of leadership felt heavier than ever. "What if I'm leading us into a trap?" he asked. "What if we fail and the lands are lost because of me?"

Gronkar stepped forward, his voice gruff but steady. "You're doing what no one else could, Kairos. Grimbold trusted you, and we trust you too. You've got this."

For a moment, Kairos let the silence stretch between them, letting their words sink in. He looked at Otona and Gronkar, seeing the exhaustion in their faces but also the unwavering belief they had in him. He couldn't let his doubts break him—not now.

"We need to be prepared for whatever comes next," Kairos said, his voice firmer now. "Lethiriel's retreat means she's planning something. We'll stay on guard."

Otona nodded. "She's after more than just the Seed. She knows something we don't, and until we figure out what that is, we'll need to stay ahead of her."

Kairos stood up straighter, finally letting go of the doubt that had gnawed at him. "We need to protect the Seed and finish what Grimbold started. No matter what Lethiriel throws at us, we'll find a way."

Gronkar grunted in agreement, but he still had a fiery gleam in his eye. "Next time, though, we finish it. No more games."

The group shared a brief moment of quiet as the wind whistled through the valley. They were bruised, bloodied, and weary, but they had survived. Kairos glanced back at the path ahead—The real battle still awaits us.

"Let's keep moving," Kairos said. "We need to get back to the new lands."

The Seed pulsed softly in his hand, a reminder of the responsibility they carried. Despite their doubts, they knew they had no choice but to press on. With renewed determination, they began their journey once more, leaving the battle behind but carrying its scars with them.

Chapter 11

The air in the valley was thick with tension as Kairos, Otona, and Gronkar pressed forward, their steps careful and deliberate. The encounter with Lethiriel still lingered in their minds, and though they had narrowly escaped with the Seed of Life, none of them believed they were out of danger. They moved swiftly yet cautiously, aware that Lethiriel's mercenaries could still be following them.

Kairos felt the weight of the Seed of Life growing heavier with each step, as if the ancient artifact was reacting to the land around them. It pulsed faintly in his pack, casting a warm, golden light through the fabric. Every now and then, he glanced behind them, feeling that they weren't alone.

Otona led the way, her eyes sharp and vigilant, scanning the path ahead for any sign of danger. Gronkar walked beside her, his usually loud presence now subdued by a gnawing frustration. They had survived Lethiriel's ambush, but the threat still loomed large over them.

"We need to stay ahead of them," Otona whispered as they reached a small ridge overlooking the dense forest below. "Lethiriel won't just give up. She'll send her people after us again if she thinks she can catch us off guard."

Gronkar grunted, gripping the hilt of his Warhammer tightly. "We can't keep running forever. At some point, we'll have to face them again."

Kairos listened to their exchange, feeling the pressure of leadership pressing down on him. They had the Seed, but it wasn't just Lethiriel they had to worry about now. The shapeshifter was still out there, lurking in the shadows, waiting for the right moment to strike.

"We'll take the ridge and follow the tree line. It'll give us better cover," Kairos suggested, glancing at the terrain ahead. The path would be rough, but it was better than staying exposed in the open valley where they could be ambushed.

Otona nodded, already moving toward the trees. "It'll slow us down a bit, but it's safer than the main trail. If Lethiriel's mercenaries are tracking us, they'll expect us to take the easiest route."

As they moved into the forest, the atmosphere shifted. The forest felt alive, almost as if it was watching them. Every crack of a branch or rustle of leaves set them on edge. The Seed of Life pulsed brighter in Kairos' pack, and he couldn't shake the feeling that it was trying to warn them.

Gronkar glanced over at Kairos, noticing his unease. "That thing... it's reacting to something, isn't it?" he asked, his voice low.

Kairos nodded, feeling the faint vibration of the Seed's magic. "I don't know what it is, but something is setting it off. We need to stay alert."

They continued forward, the forest growing thicker around them, the light from the Seed of Life casting faint shadows on the ground. Every step felt heavier than the last, the air charged with the kind of tension that only came before a storm.

"We have to be close," Otona whispered, though even she sounded uncertain. "Let's hope Lethiriel's not following us."

But Kairos wasn't so sure. He could feel the presence of something dangerous on the horizon, something far worse than Lethiriel's pursuit. The Seed of Life's power was resonating with the land, and Kairos knew that the shapeshifter was still out there...somewhere.

The further they traveled, the more unsettling the land became. What had once been lush and vibrant from the magic of the new lands was now showing signs of decay. The ground beneath their feet cracked in jagged lines, splitting open like wounds. The air felt thick and heavy, as if it were pressing down on them, making every breath feel labored. Otona was the first to notice the shift, her sharp eyes catching the subtle signs of something wrong.

"Something's not right here," Otona said, her voice barely above a whisper as she scanned the area around them. "The land... it's changing."

Kairos stopped walking and glanced around, sensing the same thing. The vibrant magic of the new lands had become unstable, its energy distorted. The Seed of Life in his pack pulsed erratically, its golden glow flickering as if warning them of the growing danger.

Gronkar tensed, gripping his Warhammer. "I don't like this. The ground feels wrong... like it's alive and waiting to swallow us whole."

As they moved forward, strange creatures watched them from the shadows—small, twisted beings with glowing eyes, lurking just beyond the tree line. Though they kept their distance, their presence made the group uneasy.

Otona crouched by the cracked earth, running her fingers along the fractures. "These fractures can't be good for these lands. The land is reacting to something. I think it's the Seed."

Kairos frowned, feeling the weight of the Seed more intensely than ever. "The Seed's power is connected to the land, but... this feels like more than that."

The wind picked up, carrying with it faint whispers of dark magic, the kind that sent chills down their spines. Kairos instinctively touched the Seed, feeling its warmth battling against the cold energy that surrounded them. He could sense the presence of something—no, someone—far more dangerous lurking nearby.

"The shapeshifter," Otona muttered, her eyes narrowing. "It's feeding off the chaos. I can feel it—like it's using the instability of the land to get stronger."

Gronkar clenched his jaw. "If that thing's getting stronger, we need to move faster. We can't let it catch us out here."

Kairos nodded, though his mind was racing with thoughts of the shapeshifter and Lethiriel's cryptic warnings. Every step they took brought them closer to the heart of the new lands, but also closer to the source of this growing darkness. The Seed's erratic glow seemed to pulse in time with the land's instability, as if it were struggling to hold back the corruption spreading around them.

"We don't have much time," Kairos said, his voice filled with urgency. "The shapeshifter's close. We need to reach the new lands and use the Seed before it's too late."

Otona's gaze was hard as she stood and gripped her bow tightly. "Then let's not waste another second."

They pressed forward, the land cracking and shifting beneath them, the weight of their mission growing heavier with each step. The shapeshifter's influence was spreading, and they could feel its eyes on them, lurking in the darkness, waiting for the right moment to strike.

But they couldn't stop now. Not when the fate of the new lands—and possibly all of Mulvyon—rested on their shoulders.

As the group continued their tense journey, the air around them seemed to warp. The vibrant colors of the valley faded into muted tones, and the ground beneath their feet shifted, as if the land itself was alive. Kairos could feel it in his bones—the shapeshifter was close, far closer than they had anticipated.

"The land... it's twisting," Gronkar said, his voice low and filled with unease. "Something's playing with us."

Kairos nodded, his eyes scanning the landscape. The path ahead looked normal, but every instinct in his body screamed that something was wrong. "Stay close. Whatever this is, it's meant to confuse us."

Suddenly, the sky darkened, and a thick mist rolled in, swallowing the horizon. Otona gasped as the path ahead splintered into several, each one looking just as real as the next. "Which one is real?" she muttered, gripping her bow tightly.

Before Kairos could answer, a voice echoed through the fog—a voice that sounded like his own. "Are you sure you're the leader they need, Kairos?" it whispered mockingly. "Do you really think you can save anyone?"

Kairos froze, his heart racing. The voice cut deep, striking at the core of his insecurities. He had doubted his ability to lead ever since the journey began, and now, the shapeshifter was using those doubts against him.

"Otona! Gronkar!" Kairos shouted, trying to pull his companions together. But when he turned, they were gone. Panic gripped him as he spun in place, searching for them in the mist. "Otona! Gronkar! Where are you?"

No answer. Only silence, followed by more whispers. This time, the voices came from every direction, as if the fog itself was alive, surrounding him, suffocating him. "You're not strong enough. You can't protect them. They'll die because of you."

Meanwhile, Otona found herself lost in a vision of her own. She was standing in the middle of the elven stronghold, the familiar sight of her mother, Alara, looming over her. Alara's cold eyes burned with the same disdain as the day she had cast Otona out. "You're nothing but an outcast," Alara's voice said, sharp and cutting. "A freak. No one will ever trust you."

Otona's heart clenched as the words hit her. She had spent her life trying to prove her worth, but deep down, those wounds never truly healed. The shapeshifter was drawing on her deepest fears, pulling her into a spiral of doubt.

Gronkar, too, was trapped in his own nightmare. He was back on the boat, the sirens' haunting melody filling his ears. Their voices, sweet and irresistible, echoed in his mind, reminding him of his failure. "You were weak. You almost drowned them all." The weight of that guilt bore down on him, and for a moment, he couldn't tell if he was still on solid ground or sinking back into those dark waters.

The illusions worked their magic, pulling each of them into their own fears and insecurities. The shapeshifter wasn't just a physical threat—it was a master of manipulation, preying on their vulnerabilities, trying to tear them apart from within.

Kairos, though, felt something stir inside him—a small flicker of defiance. The fog closed in, the voices louder, but he forced himself to focus. He gripped the Seed of Life in his pack, feeling its warmth spread through his fingers. It was a reminder of why they were here, of the mission they had sworn to complete.

"This isn't real," he whispered to himself, then louder: "This isn't real!"

He clenched his fists and shouted into the mist, his voice cutting through the chaos. "Enough! We won't fall for your tricks!"

In an instant, the fog began to thin. Kairos could see faint shapes ahead—Otona and Gronkar, both caught in their own nightmares. He ran toward them, shaking them from their trances. "Otona! Gronkar, snap out of it! This is all an illusion!"

Otona blinked, the vision of her mother fading as Kairos' voice reached her. She shook her head, breaking free of the shapeshifter's grip. Gronkar, still shaken, stumbled backward, the sound of the sirens fading from his ears.

"The shapeshifter..." Otona muttered, still recovering from the vision. "It's trying to break us."

"But it won't," Kairos said, his voice firm. "We're stronger than this."

The illusions faded completely, the fog lifting as the group regrouped, their breaths heavy but determined. The shapeshifter's influence had come close to breaking them, but Kairos' resolve had brought them back from the edge.

"Stay close," Kairos warned, his eyes narrowing as he scanned the horizon. "It's not done with us yet."

The group, shaken but unified, pressed forward, knowing that they were now playing a dangerous game with a creature that could warp reality itself. The shapeshifter's influence was growing stronger, and they would need every ounce of strength and trust in each other to survive what was coming.

The landscape around them shifted and warped, as if the very earth was under the shapeshifter's thrall. Every step felt heavier, the air thicker, making it hard to breathe. Kairos, Otona, and Gronkar pressed forward, the weight of the Seed of Life in Kairos' pack growing heavier with each passing moment. The urgency of their mission crackled in the air around them, fueling their desperation.

"We're running out of time," Otona said, her voice strained as she pushed aside a branch. She glanced up at the darkening sky. The winds had picked up, howling in a way that made it feel like the land itself was alive—and angry.

Kairos wiped sweat from his brow, glancing over at his companions. Their exhaustion was evident. They had been through so much already—facing sirens, giants, and now the shapeshifter, whose influence was growing stronger by the second. Despite the physical and emotional toll, they had no choice but to keep going.

"We can't stop," Kairos said, his voice firm though his body ached. "The longer we take, the stronger it gets. It feeds on our fear... our doubts." He had finally understood. The shapeshifter wasn't just manipulating the land around them—it was feeding on the group's uncertainty, growing more powerful with every moment they hesitated.

"Fear," Otona repeated, her brow furrowing as she tried to keep up with Kairos' pace. "That's how it's gaining strength."

Gronkar, lagging slightly behind, grunted in frustration. "Then we'd better move faster. If that thing's feeding on our fear, we've given it enough to grow into a monster."

Kairos looked back at Gronkar, seeing the truth in his words. They had all been afraid, each of them haunted by their own insecurities, but now was the time to push through it. They had to find the strength to finish this, no matter how daunting the task.

As they pressed on, the ground beneath them trembled, cracks splintering through the earth. Unstable patches of dirt shifted beneath their feet, threatening to swallow them at any moment. The trees groaned as violent winds tore through the valley, bending and twisting them in unnatural ways. Every step forward felt like a battle against the elements themselves.

The Seed of Life, strapped to Kairos' back, began to pulse faintly, almost as if sensing the growing danger. Its glow flickered in rhythm with the chaos around them, a warning of just how critical their mission was.

"The land... it's reacting to the Seed," Otona said, her eyes narrowing as she noticed the pulsing light. "It's almost like it knows what's at stake."

Kairos nodded. "And the shapeshifter knows it too. We're getting closer. It's trying to stop us." He glanced at the crumbling path ahead, a jagged and twisted route that would take them closer to the new lands, but at the cost of navigating the volatile terrain.

Gronkar pushed forward, determined. "Let it try," he growled. "We've come too far to turn back now."

Despite their fatigue, the group forced themselves onward. The winds howled louder, carrying whispers of the shapeshifter's voice—taunting them, mocking them. Every step forward felt like a struggle, but they refused to stop. They couldn't stop.

As they approached the border of the new lands, the environment only grew more chaotic. The sky above them churned, clouds swirling in ominous patterns, as if reflecting the storm that was brewing in their minds. Kairos could feel the shapeshifter's presence more strongly now, lurking just beyond the horizon. It was waiting for them.

"We're almost there," Kairos said, though his voice lacked its usual confidence. He wasn't sure what awaited them once they crossed into the new lands, but he knew one thing for certain—they would need every ounce of strength they had left to face what was coming.

With the Seed of Life glowing brightly at his back, Kairos clenched his fists and led his companions into the storm.

The ground trembled beneath their feet as the group pressed forward, the twisted landscape of the new lands looming ahead. The air crackled with an eerie tension, as though the very world was holding its breath, waiting for something to break. Every step they took felt heavier, laden with the weight of what they had seen, what they had lost, and what still lay ahead.

Kairos, Otona, and Gronkar trudged onward, their bodies exhausted but their minds alert, the Seed of Life glowing steadily at Kairos' back. The light from the Seed, once calming, now seemed almost desperate, as if it, too, was aware of the growing danger that threatened everything.

Kairos couldn't shake the feeling that something was wrong. The shapeshifter's power had grown—he could feel it—and it wasn't just about controlling the new lands anymore. The deeper they ventured, the clearer it became that the shapeshifter's ambitions were far greater than they had ever imagined.

Suddenly, Otona stopped, her eyes narrowing as she gazed at the horizon. "Do you feel that?" she asked, her voice hushed.

Gronkar, usually the one to dismiss concerns, nodded grimly. "It's everywhere... the land, the air. It's... wrong."

Kairos tightened his grip on the straps of his pack. The Seed of Life pulsed brightly, its energy reacting to the dark magic that swirled around them. He exchanged a glance with Otona, who nodded in silent agreement. Whatever was happening, it was bigger than they had anticipated.

As they continued walking, a realization struck Kairos with the force of a tidal wave. "It's not just about the new lands," he muttered, his voice heavy with dread. "The shapeshifter... it's using the chaos of the new lands to spread its influence."

Otona turned to him, her expression grave. "What do you mean?"

Kairos' thoughts raced as the pieces began to fall into place. "The instability here—it's just the beginning. The shapeshifter doesn't just want control over these lands... it wants all of Mulvyon. It wants to reshape the entire world in Tythalor's image. If it gains enough power, it could plunge everything into chaos. All the races, all the lands... none of it will survive."

A cold silence fell over the group as the weight of Kairos' words sank in. Otona and Gronkar exchanged a worried look, both of them processing the magnitude of what Kairos was saying.

"Grimbold knew," Kairos continued, his voice cracking with emotion. "That's why he sacrificed himself. He knew it was more than just about the new lands. The Seed of Life... it's not just a way to restore balance. It's the only thing that can stop the shapeshifter from spreading its corruption across all of Mulvyon."

Gronkar clenched his fists, his voice tight with anger. "So, this thing... it wants to turn the world into another version of Tythalor's evil? That's why it's been toying with us... feeding on our fears."

Otona nodded slowly, the realization dawning in her eyes. "This isn't just about saving the new lands anymore. This is about stopping the shapeshifter from destroying everything."

For a moment, none of them spoke. The enormity of the situation weighed heavily on their shoulders, more than they had ever expected to face. They weren't just fighting for a single land—they were fighting for the fate of the entire world.

Kairos took a deep breath, his resolve hardening. "We have to stop it. Whatever it takes. Grimbold gave everything to protect the Seed, and we can't let his sacrifice be in vain."

Otona placed a hand on Kairos' shoulder, her eyes filled with fierce determination. "We're with you, Kairos. Whatever comes next, we'll face it together."

Gronkar grunted in agreement, his usual bravado tempered by the gravity of the moment. "We've come too far to give up now."

Kairos nodded, feeling the weight of their loyalty and trust. The shapeshifter was growing stronger, and the final battle was drawing near. But for the first time, he felt a sense of clarity. This was their mission—this was what they had been fighting for all along.

As the twisted landscape of the new lands stretched out before them, the group knew that their greatest challenge still lay ahead. They were not just returning the Seed of Life—they were preparing for the final conflict, a battle that would determine the future of all Mulvyon and the entire world.

With renewed determination, they pressed on, their minds focused and their hearts united.

Chapter 12

The group moved cautiously as they moved through the new lands. What had once been an untouched landscape—lush forests, rivers, and fertile fields—was now a twisted version of itself. The land had become wild and chaotic, distorted by the lingering presence of dark magic. Trees grew unnaturally tall, their branches twisting like claws. The ground beneath their feet seemed to pulse with an unstable energy, and the sky was a mix of swirling gray clouds, as if even the heavens had been disturbed.

The Seed of Life, in Kairos' care, glowed with an intense light, pulsing in rhythm with the erratic landscape. It was as if the Seed was reacting to the instability, urging them to move forward. The magic it contained felt alive, vibrating with power and purpose, but it also seemed fragile, as if the wrong move could cause the entire balance to shatter.

Otona, eyes scanning the horizon, moved silently beside Kairos, her bow ready. Gronkar marched on the other side, his usually confident expression replaced with a mix of wariness and frustration. His eyes flicked from one twisted tree to another, clearly unsettled by the unnatural growth around them.

"This place has changed... It's worse than before," Otona murmured, her voice low but tense.

"It's the shapeshifter," Kairos said. "It's using the chaos in the land to grow stronger, feeding off the instability." He could feel the weight of leadership more than ever now. They were so close to the end, but the danger had only grown. The land itself was a threat.

Grimbold's sacrifice echoed in his mind. The old centaur had given everything to protect them and ensure that the Seed would make it back to the heart of the new lands. Now it was up to them to finish the task.

"The Seed feels heavier than before," Kairos admitted, his voice laced with exhaustion. "As if it's drawing in the magic of the land around us."

Gronkar frowned, glancing at the glowing Seed. "It wants to be planted, doesn't it? It knows this place is falling apart."

Otona nodded in agreement, her gaze sweeping across the eerie terrain. "The land is sick. If we don't get the Seed to the heart of the new lands soon, it might be too late."

As they ventured deeper, the atmosphere became more oppressive. The air itself seemed to vibrate with dark energy, and they could feel the shapeshifter's presence lurking just beyond their sight, always watching, always waiting. Each step forward was a struggle against the weight of uncertainty and dread.

"Stay sharp," Kairos said, his voice steady but tense. "The shapeshifter is here. We just can't see it yet."

The others nodded, and they pressed on, their steps heavier as they marched toward the heart of the new lands, knowing that the final battle was coming.

The deeper the group ventured into the new lands, the more twisted and unnatural everything became. Trees with blackened bark and warped branches seemed to lean in toward them, as if watching. The ground felt unstable, pulsing beneath their feet with dark energy that seemed to mirror the magic around them. The once beautiful land was now a perverse shadow of its former self, corrupted by the shapeshifter's influence.

Kairos led the way, the Seed of Life glowing, a constant reminder of their purpose. Its light flickered with each step, reacting to the growing instability. Otona and Gronkar moved cautiously beside him, their weapons drawn, eyes scanning the unnatural surroundings.

Suddenly, Otona froze. "We're not alone," she said in a low, urgent whisper, her sharp gaze locking onto something in the distance. Her bow was already raised, an arrow notched, ready for whatever was lurking in the shadows.

Without warning, the ground began to rumble. From the earth, monstrous creatures emerged—mutated beasts, once normal animals but now grotesquely twisted by dark magic. Wolves with extra limbs, stags whose antlers had grown sharp like blades, and—most horrifying of all—massive, mutated scorpions that skittered toward them with terrifying speed.

The scorpions' carapaces gleamed with a sickly sheen; their pincers sharp enough to crush bone. They moved unnaturally fast for their size, their long tails tipped with venomous stingers that glowed faintly in the dim light. Their many legs clicked across the rocky ground, creating a nightmarish chorus that sent a chill through the group.

"Scorpions! Watch out!" Gronkar shouted, swinging his Warhammer with a grunt of effort. He brought it crashing down on the nearest beast, smashing its tail into the dirt just before it could strike.

But for every creature they felled, more took its place. The air was thick with the scent of decay, and the ground beneath them seemed to writhe as though it, too, had been infected by the shapeshifter's magic.

A wolf-like creature lunged at Kairos, its jaws snapping viciously. He dodged, slicing its throat with his twin daggers, but he barely had time to recover before a massive scorpion lunged at him, its stinger aimed for his heart.

Kairos rolled to the side just in time, narrowly avoiding the deadly tail as it embedded itself into the earth where he had laid. The creature's pincers snapped, and Kairos slashed at its underbelly, driving one of his daggers deep into the soft flesh between its armor-like plates. The scorpion let out a high-pitched screech, twitching violently as it collapsed to the ground.

Beside him, Otona let loose arrow after arrow, her sharp eyes targeting the weak points in the creatures' mutated forms. She downed a wolf with a precise shot to the eye, but a scorpion skittered toward her with terrifying speed. She jumped back, narrowly avoiding its stinger as it whipped past her. In one fluid motion, she notched another arrow and fired it directly into the scorpion's exposed joint, crippling its movement.

Gronkar, meanwhile, was in the thick of the fight, battling two of the scorpions at once. His Warhammer came down with bone-crushing force, shattering one of the scorpions' legs and sending it reeling. But the second scorpion lunged at him from behind, its pincers catching him across the arm, drawing blood. Gronkar growled in pain but didn't falter, using his brute strength to twist free and slam his hammer into the creature's side, sending it crashing to the ground.

"They're endless!" Gronkar shouted, blood dripping down his arm, his eyes wild with frustration.

Kairos could feel the pressure mounting. They were being overwhelmed. The shapeshifter's creatures were too many, and they seemed to grow stronger the deeper they pushed into the new lands. For every beast they killed, more emerged from the shadows, mutated scorpions leading the charge with their venomous stingers and sharp pincers.

Kairos wiped sweat from his brow, his muscles aching from the constant onslaught. He saw Otona narrowly avoid another scorpion, her face a mask of grim determination. Gronkar, though bleeding, fought with a ferocity that matched the creatures' wild attacks. But he could see the fatigue setting in—on all of them.

As if sensing their desperation, the Seed of Life began to glow brighter, pulsing in Kairos' pack like a heartbeat. Its light cut through the darkness around them, and for a moment, the creatures seemed to hesitate, their movements slowing.

"We need to push through! Get to the heart of the new lands before they overwhelm us!" Kairos shouted.

But just as they regained some control over the battles, the largest of the scorpions—a hulking creature twice the size of the others, with armor-like plating covering its entire body—emerged from the earth, its tail dripping with venom. It charged toward them with terrifying speed.

Otona, quick as ever, loosed an arrow that ricocheted harmlessly off its shell.

"It's too strong!" she called out, her voice edged with panic. "We need to find another way!"

Kairos darted forward, narrowly avoiding the scorpion's deadly stinger as it struck the ground beside him. He knew they had to finish this, but the battles were pushing them to their limits. If they couldn't defeat the shapeshifter's creatures here, they might not survive the journey to the heart of the new lands.

With one final surge of determination, Kairos signaled to Otona and Gronkar, their silent understanding clear. Together, they launched one last, coordinated attack, using every ounce of strength and skill they had left to take down the remaining creatures.

As the final scorpion fell, its body twitching in death, the group collapsed to the ground, panting and covered in dirt and blood. They had survived, but barely.

The group stood at the edge of the heart of the new lands, and what lay before them was beyond anything they had imagined. The earth pulsed beneath their feet, the ground shifting in waves as if it were alive. Trees twisted and warped, growing and shrinking in size within moments. Rivers of magic flowed like molten light through the air, the land itself glowing with the unstable energy of the shapeshifter's dark influence.

"This is it," Kairos whispered, his voice barely audible over the roar of the magic surging around them. The Seed of Life, its light pulsing in rhythm with the shifting landscape.

The others gathered beside Karios, their expressions mirroring the gravity of the moment. Otona scanned the surroundings warily, her bow ready, while Gronkar stood with his Warhammer slung over his shoulder, though even he seemed unsure of how brute strength could help in a place like this.

"The land's alive here," Gronkar muttered. "Feels like it's trying to throw us off."

"The shapeshifter's doing, no doubt," Otona replied, her eyes narrowing at the ever-changing environment. "We'll have to move carefully. If we push too hard, the ground could swallow us whole."

Gronkar grunted in disagreement, his frustration boiling beneath the surface. "Or we push through and get this done. The longer we wait, the worse this gets."

Kairos feeling the weight of responsibility heavier than ever. He knew Gronkar wasn't wrong—time was running out, and the shapeshifter's influence was growing stronger with each passing moment. But he also knew Otona's caution was warranted. One wrong move could destroy everything they had fought for.

"Both of you are right," Kairos said, his voice steady despite the chaos around them. "But we have to follow the Seed's guidance. It'll show us the way."

As if in response to his words, the Seed began to glow brighter, its light flickering and pulsing like a heartbeat. The air around it shimmered, and for the briefest moment, the chaotic land seemed to calm. A path, faint but visible, appeared before them, winding through the unstable terrain.

"There," Kairos said, pointing to the glowing path. "That's where we need to go."

Otona eyed the shifting ground warily. "It's not stable. We'll need to move fast, or the land could shift again and trap us."

Gronkar flexed his hands around his Warhammer, ready for action. "Fast, I can do."

The group began to move, following the path illuminated by the Seed. The ground beneath their feet trembled, and the air crackled with raw magic, but the Seed's light guided them, steady and unwavering.

Kairos kept his focus on the Seed, feeling its power surge through him, urging him forward.

As they ventured deeper into the heart of the new lands, the chaos around them grew more intense. The earth buckled and twisted, and the air hummed with the shapeshifter's influence. It was as though the very land was fighting back, resisting the Seed's power.

"We're close," Otona said, her voice tense with anticipation. "I can feel it."

Kairos nodded, but the weight in his chest grew heavier with every step. They were nearing the center of the new lands, the place where the Seed of Life needed to be planted to restore balance. But something dark and menacing lurked in the air—a presence they couldn't see, but that Kairos knew was watching them.

As they approached the final stretch of the path, the Seed of Life began to pulse even more intensely, its glow casting a golden light over the land. The ground before them shifted and cracked, but the path remained, leading them to a small clearing where the magic was at its most concentrated.

"This is it," Kairos said, stopping at the edge of the clearing. "This is where we plant the Seed."

The group gathered around, each of them feeling the weight of the moment. Otona's bow was still in her hands, her sharp eyes scanning the surroundings for any signs of danger. Gronkar, though clearly exhausted from the journey, stood ready to defend them if needed.

Kairos knelt at the center of the clearing; the Seed of Life glowing brightly in his hands. The air hummed with magic, and for the first time since they had entered the new lands, there was a moment of stillness—a moment where it felt like they might succeed.

But as Kairos prepared to plant the Seed, a chilling gust of wind swept through the clearing, carrying with it a whisper of darkness.

"I was wondering when you'd arrive," a voice hissed from the shadows.

Kairos' heart sank as he rose to his feet, turning toward the source of the voice. The shapeshifter had returned.

Just as Kairos lowered the Seed of Life toward the shifting ground, the air seemed to freeze. A biting cold slithered through the valley, carrying with it a voice that dripped with malice and ancient power.

"Did you truly believe I would let you succeed?"

The group froze, their instincts sharpening as the darkness at the edge of the clearing seemed to thicken, swirling unnaturally. Slowly, from the shadows, the shapeshifter emerged, more grotesque and dangerous than ever before. Its form flickered between each of the group members—Kairos, Otona, Gronkar—before finally shifting into a twisted version of Grimbold.

But something was different this time. The shapeshifter's form began to ripple, its body distorting as though it were struggling to maintain its stolen shapes. Then, with a chilling hiss, the creature morphed into something far more terrifying—a shape beyond human or beast, a true manifestation of its chaotic nature.

The creature's true form was monstrous. It stood taller than any of them, its body a grotesque fusion of shadow, sinew, and glistening black scales. Jagged horns curled from its head, and its glowing red eyes burned with malevolent intelligence. Its hands were long, clawed, and dripping with a dark, oily substance. The air around it pulsed with an oppressive magic, thick and suffocating.

"Now," the shapeshifter's voice echoed, deeper and more commanding, "you will face the true me."

Kairos tightened his grip on his dagger, but the creature was faster than he expected. In a blur of movement, the shapeshifter lunged at him, claws slashing through the air. Kairos barely had time to dodge, but the shapeshifter's speed and power were unmatched. Its clawed hand struck Kairos across the face, ripping through skin and leaving a deep, jagged scar. He staggered back, clutching his face as hot blood poured from the wound.

"Kairos!" Otona shouted, her eyes wide with horror.

Kairos gritted his teeth, ignoring the searing pain. His vision blurred, but he refused to fall. He could feel the warm blood dripping down his face, but he forced himself to stand tall, dagger ready.

The shapeshifter let out a low, mocking laugh, its red eyes gleaming with sadistic delight. "You're weak, Kairos. You can't lead them. You can't even protect yourself."

Before Kairos could respond, the shapeshifter turned on Otona, its body moving with inhuman speed. It lashed out with its claws, but Otona dodged, rolling across the ground and firing a quick volley of arrows. They pierced the shapeshifter's form, but the creature merely hissed and yanked the arrows out, its wounds sealing as fast as they were made.

"You're nothing but an outcast," the shapeshifter taunted, its voice shifting to mimic Otona's own. "A freak. No one wanted you then, and no one wants you now."

Otona's face hardened, but she didn't let the words get to her. She released another volley, this time aiming for the creature's glowing eyes. The shapeshifter swerved to avoid the arrows, but the distraction gave Gronkar the opening he needed. With a roar, the beast-man charged forward, swinging his Warhammer with all his might. The weapon slammed into the creature's side, sending it skidding across the ground.

But the shapeshifter recovered quickly, faster than they expected. Its body contorted, bones cracking and reshaping as it rose to its full height. In its true form, it was nearly unstoppable.

"You think brute force will stop me, beast?" The shapeshifter sneered, its voice dripping with contempt.

Gronkar roared again, charging forward, but the shapeshifter was ready. It ducked under Gronkar's next strike and delivered a vicious slash to his back, sending him crashing to the ground. Gronkar groaned in pain, struggling to rise, but the shapeshifter was relentless, raining blow after blow on him.

Otona fired another arrow, trying to draw the creature's attention, but it was far more skilled in its true form. It dodged easily, its movements fluid and deadly. Kairos, his face still bleeding and vision clouded by pain, forced himself into action. With a desperate cry, he lunged at the shapeshifter, slashing with his dagger.

The shapeshifter spun around, blocking Kairos' attack with ease. "Pathetic," it growled, grabbing him by the throat and lifting him into the air. Kairos gasped, his vision darkening as the creature's grip tightened around his neck.

"Your journey ends here," the shapeshifter hissed, its red eyes glowing with triumph.

But as the creature prepared to deliver the killing blow, Kairos felt the Seed of Life pulse in his hand. A burst of energy surged through him, giving him the strength to break free from the shapeshifter's grasp. He slashed at its arm, causing the creature to roar in pain and drop him.

Kairos fell to the ground, coughing and gasping for air, but he wasted no time. He scrambled to his feet, gripping the Seed of Life tightly. The creature, enraged by the attack, charged at him once more, but Kairos was ready.

"Otona! Gronkar! Now!" Kairos shouted.

The group moved as one. Gronkar swung his Warhammer with all his might, slamming it into the shapeshifter's side, while Otona fired her arrows with deadly precision. The shapeshifter staggered under the combined assault, but it was still far from defeated.

As the shapeshifter roared in pain, its form flickering and shifting in and out of focus, Kairos knew this was their moment. He tightened his grip on the Seed of Life, feeling its powerful energy pulsating through his hand. He could sense the land beneath them crying out for balance, and he knew that planting the Seed was their only hope. The shapeshifter's chaotic influence was everywhere, but the Seed had the power to set things right.

"Otona, Gronkar!" Kairos shouted over the deafening roar of the battle. "I need you both to keep it busy. I'm going to plant the Seed."

Without hesitation, Otona and Gronkar sprang into action. Otona nocked an arrow, her sharp eyes locked onto the shapeshifter. She loosed arrow after arrow, each one aimed at its shifting form, forcing the creature to react and defend itself. Gronkar, despite the deep wounds on his back from the shapeshifter's claws, charged forward with a war cry, swinging his Warhammer with all his might. His strength and determination were unwavering, even as blood dripped from his back.

"I've got your back, Kairos!" Gronkar growled, his voice strained from the pain, but his resolve unshaken.

Kairos moved quickly, kneeling beside the twisting earth where the Seed needed to be planted. The ground seemed alive, constantly shifting and pulsing with chaotic magic. He could feel the energy thrumming beneath him, wild and unpredictable. But as he held the Seed in his hands, its warmth spread through him, filling him with a sense of calm and purpose.

"Otona, watch his left!" Gronkar yelled as he parried a savage strike from the shapeshifter, his muscles straining against the creature's unnatural strength.

Otona dodged to the side, rolling across the ground and loosing another arrow mid-dive. The shapeshifter hissed in frustration, its flickering form taking on Otona's own face for a split second, trying to mock her. "You're an outcast, Otona," it sneered in her voice. "No one wanted you—no one will ever want you."

But Otona didn't flinch. She fired another arrow, her face hard with determination. "Your words are nothing," she spat. "You can't break me."

The shapeshifter's form shimmered, its confidence waning. The more it tried to taunt and manipulate them, the less effective it became. Its power had thrived on their doubts, their fears, but now—now there was no fear left. They knew who they were, and they knew what they were fighting for.

Kairos could feel the shapeshifter's weakening presence. The Seed pulsed stronger in his hand, reacting to the fading chaos around them. He dug his hand into the earth, feeling the life force beneath the surface. This was it. He could save the new lands. He could stop the shapeshifter once and for all.

"Kairos, hurry!" Otona shouted, her voice laced with urgency. Gronkar grunted in pain, but still, he swung his Warhammer with unrelenting force. "We're not sure how much longer we can hold it off!"

"I'm almost there!" Kairos shouted back, his heart racing. He pressed the Seed into the earth, his hands trembling as the magic began to surge through him.

The moment the Seed touched the soil, a bright light erupted from the ground. It spread out in waves, rolling through the landscape like a tidal wave of energy. The land around them glowed with vibrant life, the chaotic magic retreating as the Seed's power restored balance to the world.

The shapeshifter screamed, its form twisting and writhing in agony. The light of the Seed was too much for it—its dark magic couldn't survive in the presence of such pure, untainted life. It lashed out one final time, desperate to stop them, but it was too late. The Seed had taken root.

As the light from the Seed grew brighter, the shapeshifter's form began to break apart. Its body crumbled into shadowy tendrils that were sucked back into the earth, swallowed by the power of the Seed. Kairos, Otona, and Gronkar stood their ground, watching as the creature dissolved before their eyes.

Finally, with one last anguished shriek, the shapeshifter vanished completely, leaving only silence in its wake.

Kairos collapsed onto his knees, exhausted but filled with relief. He had done it. They had done it. The Seed of Life was planted, and the land would heal.

Otona rushed to Gronkar's side, her face pale as she noticed the deep gashes across his back. "You're hurt," she said, worry creeping into her voice.

Gronkar winced but offered a weak grin. "Just a scratch," he said, though his voice was strained. "It'll take more than that to bring me down."

Kairos stood slowly, wiping the blood from his face where the shapeshifter had scarred him. The mark would be a permanent reminder of this battle, but it was one he would wear with pride. He looked at the spot where the shapeshifter had disappeared, knowing that the battle had not only been physical but also a test of their inner strength.

Together, they had overcome their doubts and fears. Together, they had planted the Seed.

As the light from the Seed began to spread, filling the new lands with hope and life, Kairos, Otona, and Gronkar stood side by side, ready for whatever challenges lay ahead.

The ground beneath Kairos' feet pulsed with the steady hum of magic as the Seed of Life took root in the heart of the new lands. A blinding light shot up from where he had planted it, spreading across the landscape like ripples in water. The once chaotic, twisted land began to heal before their eyes. Trees grew tall and strong, rivers started to flow with clear water, and the air itself felt fresher—cleaner.

Kairos nodded, though the weight of the journey was still heavy on his shoulders. "The shapeshifter's gone," he said, looking at the place where their enemy had stood. "But it feels... bittersweet."

The land around them was transforming, the Seed of Life's power spreading like a wave of renewal. The vibrant green grass that grew where once barren earth had been was a stark contrast to the twisted, cursed land it had been. Trees, once blackened and corrupt, now flourished with life. But despite the beauty of the restoration, a shadow of loss hung over them.

"Grimbold should be here," Otona said softly, her eyes misting as she gazed at the new life around them. "He deserved to see this."

Gronkar grunted in agreement, wiping the sweat and blood from his brow. "He gave everything for this. We owe him our lives."

But as those words settled, something extraordinary happened. From the center of where the Seed was planted, the pulsing light shifted, brightening until it became a beam of pure white energy. The group took a cautious step back, startled as the air shimmered with magic. The Seed, glowing with life, began to release a soft, ethereal mist, swirling upward. And from that mist, a familiar figure began to emerge—Grimbold.

His form wasn't solid but a translucent, radiant spirit. His eyes, filled with the wisdom and weariness of his long life, now sparkled with a peaceful glow. He stood tall; his spectral form no longer bound by the limitations of his old body. For a moment, the entire valley was silent, the gentle breeze carrying his presence toward them.

Kairos, Otona, and Gronkar stared in awe, barely able to believe what they were seeing.

"Grimbold..." Kairos whispered; his voice heavy with emotion.

The spirit of the centaur warrior smiled at them, the lines of his face soft and at peace. "You have done well," Grimbold's voice echoed, calm and resonant like the wind itself. "The Seed is planted. The balance is restored."

Otona took a step forward, her voice trembling. "But you're... You're free now?"

Grimbold nodded slowly. "My duty is fulfilled. The Seed of Life needed its guardian, and now that you have delivered it, my spirit can rest."

Gronkar, blinking back tears, straightened himself as best he could. "You sacrificed yourself for us, for all of this."

Grimbold's spirit tilted his head toward the newly thriving land. "It was always my purpose to protect the Seed, to ensure it would one day restore these lands. My time has ended, but yours... yours is just beginning."

Kairos swallowed the lump in his throat, stepping closer. "We couldn't have done this without you, Grimbold. We'll honor your sacrifice, I promise."

The centaur's spirit gazed at them with pride. "You already have, Kairos. Each of you. You stood strong in the face of darkness. But know this—the path ahead will still be filled with trials. The land is healing, but the world is still fragile. Protect it. Guard it. And know that I will watch over you."

The light around Grimbold began to intensify, his figure slowly dissolving into the mist as his spirit found its peace.

Otona, her voice barely above a whisper, said, "Thank you, Grimbold. For everything."

The last remnants of his form shimmered in the light, his final words echoing softly in the wind. "May the land always guide your steps."

And then, Grimbold's spirit faded, leaving behind a profound silence. The Seed of Life stood in the heart of the valley, pulsing gently with its life-giving magic, and the land around them, once twisted and dying, now breathed with new vitality.

The group stood together, their grief mingled with a sense of victory and peace. They had saved the new lands. But more than that, they had honored a hero who had given his all to restore balance.

Chapter 13

The new lands, once wracked by chaos and darkness, were beginning to heal. Everywhere Kairos, Otona, and Gronkar looked, they could see signs of life slowly returning—new saplings breaking through the scorched earth, streams bubbling where once there had been nothing but cracked, dry land. Yet, despite the visible progress, the scars left behind by the shapeshifter ran deeper than the group had anticipated.

Kairos stood near the center of a small town, watching as villagers rebuilt homes that had been destroyed in the chaos. His role as a leader, though once something he reluctantly accepted, had now solidified. Men and women came to him for guidance, seeking not only help in reconstructing their homes but in rebuilding their lives.

The burden of their expectations weighed heavily on him, just as the constant ache of his fresh scar served as a reminder of the shapeshifter's blow. The deep, jagged scar ran across his cheek and down toward his jaw. Every time he felt the sting, it reminded him of how close they had come to failing.

Not far from him, Otona worked with a group of rangers to organize the planting of crops. Her sharp eyes scanned the tree line, wary of any danger, but it was clear she struggled to adjust to this new role. As an outcast, she had lived in the shadows for so long, unsure of how to embrace this new position of respect and trust from the people.

Gronkar, despite the wounds he carried from their final battle, hauled stones and beams, helping to restore homes with his unmatched strength. His back still bore the long, jagged scars from the shapeshifter's claws, a constant reminder of the battles they had fought, but his focus was on the task at hand. He was their protector, the brawn to counterbalance Kairos' strategy and Otona's sharp precision.

Even though the Seed of Life had begun its work of healing the land, some wounds seemed impossible to mend. Fear still gripped many of the people they encountered. Families who had lost loved ones to the shapeshifter's manipulation struggled with grief. There were whispers in the air—what if the darkness returned? What if, despite their efforts, the chaos would rise again?

Kairos overheard a conversation between two villagers, a mother and father who had lost their child to the shapeshifter's influence. "We can rebuild our homes," the father said quietly, "but how do we rebuild our hearts?"

His words echoed in Kairos' mind. He touched the scar on his face absentmindedly, the pain still fresh in more ways than one. The physical rebuilding was one thing, but the emotional toll of the battle was harder to heal.

The three companions were hailed as heroes, but none of them truly felt that way. Kairos, though confident in his leadership, couldn't shake the doubts that had plagued him since the beginning. Could they have done more? Should he have made different choices? The weight of those thoughts lingered in his mind, gnawing at him, especially as he saw the haunted looks on the faces of the survivors. His scar, a mark of both victory and failure, was a constant reminder of the fine line they had walked between triumph and defeat.

Otona, too, felt the strain of her new role. She was once an outcast, driven away by her own people. Now, these people looked to her for protection and guidance. She was no longer the lone ranger stalking the wilderness. But accepting this new identity was harder than she had anticipated. She found herself standing apart from the villagers, watching them from a distance, unsure of how to fully integrate herself into this new life.

Gronkar, with his visible scars and muscular frame, was the pillar of strength that many leaned on. But inside, he was wrestling with his own demons. He had nearly been lost to the sirens' song, nearly succumbed to the shapeshifter's whispers of doubt. That shame lingered in the back of his mind, even as he carried stone after stone to help rebuild.

The land was healing, but slowly. As the Seed of Life spread its magic, the forests regrew, the rivers resumed their natural courses, and the soil became fertile again. But the process was gradual, and some areas of the land still bore the deep scars of the shapeshifter's corruption.

"We've come far," Otona said one evening, as they sat around a small fire after a long day of rebuilding. "But it's not over yet."

Kairos nodded, staring into the flames, his hand briefly touching the scar on his cheek. "It's going to take time. For all of us."

The group understood that while the shapeshifter was defeated, the journey to restore peace and balance is going to take time. There is still much to be done.

In a few weeks fresh crops rose from the once-barren soil, and villagers who had spent months in fear now dared to smile and laugh. The air buzzed with a sense of cautious relief as the people rebuilt their homes, gathered in markets, and held small festivals to celebrate their survival. Children ran through the fields, chasing each other with gleeful abandon. It was as though the world was coming back to life, piece by piece.

The mood in the towns was shifting, and it was impossible to ignore the spark of joy that had returned. In one village, music played, and colorful banners hung between freshly repaired houses. Families shared meals together, celebrating the small victories of returning to normalcy. "We survived," one villager said to Kairos, clapping him on the back. "We're alive, and the land is healing, thanks to you."

Despite the people's relief, Kairos couldn't shake a growing sense of unease. His hand absently touched the scar that ran across his face—a constant reminder of the battle with the shapeshifter and the narrow line between victory and defeat. He forced a smile and nodded to the villager, but deep inside, he felt the lingering tension of something still unfinished.

At first glance, it seemed like peace was settling over the new lands, but subtle signs hinted at a lingering darkness. Rumors began to circulate—strange, fragmented tales of nightmares plaguing those who had lived closest to the chaos. "I dream of shadows," one farmer confided to Otona as she passed through the village. "They whisper to me, telling me the darkness isn't gone, that it's just hiding."

At the edges of towns, hunters reported glimpses of creatures lurking in the woods. They were never quite able to describe what they saw—just shapes moving through the trees, too quick and too dark to be anything natural. And although the shapeshifter had been defeated, a persistent fear clung to those who had seen its horrors firsthand.

Sitting with Kairos and Otona by the fire one evening, Gronkar voiced the doubts that had been weighing on him. "It doesn't feel right," he said, staring into the flames. "We fought that thing—killed it, sure—but it felt... too easy." His voice was laced with frustration. "A creature like that doesn't just vanish like smoke. I'm telling you, there's something else at work."

Kairos nodded in agreement; his brow furrowed. The victory had been hard-won, but Gronkar's words struck a chord within him. The shapeshifter's defeat had come abruptly, as though the creature had allowed itself to be taken down—or as if its real power had not yet been revealed. The memory of the fight gnawed at him, and the growing fear that something darker still lurked in the shadows began to take root in his mind.

Otona, usually silent in these moments, spoke up. "I've noticed it too. Something is wrong." She leaned forward, her sharp eyes scanning the tree line as though expecting something to emerge. "The land is changing in ways that don't feel natural."

Kairos and Gronkar looked at her, waiting for her to explain.

"I've seen birds flying in strange patterns, moving away from their usual migrations," Otona continued. "Plants are growing faster than they should—some with twisted, unnatural shapes. And the shadows..." She trailed off, narrowing her eyes as if seeing something just beyond the fire's light. "They don't behave like they used to."

The group fell silent, the weight of Otona's observations settling over them like a cloud. They had brought balance back to the land, but it was clear that not everything had returned to normal. The darkness they had fought might have retreated, but its echoes were still present, woven into the fabric of the land itself.

The new lands, though vibrant and alive with the magic of the Seed, began to reveal strange and unsettling occurrences. At first, they seemed like isolated incidents—mere quirks of a land slowly recovering from the shapeshifter's taint—but soon, the signs became too frequent and bizarre to ignore.

Storms rolled in without warning, clouds thick and heavy with rain materializing in moments. What should have been clear, sunny skies turned dark with swirling winds and sharp, almost blinding lightning strikes. On more than one occasion, Kairos found himself staring at the sky in confusion, watching as the very air around them seemed to ripple and shift in color. Sometimes the skies turned a deep, unnatural purple or orange, casting eerie shadows across the landscape. "This isn't right," Kairos muttered, rubbing the jagged scar on his face, which tingled uncomfortably in the storm's presence.

Gronkar, ever the skeptic, narrowed his eyes. "This land was just put back together. Maybe it's trying to figure out what normal is."

Otona shook her head. "No. This feels deliberate, as if the land itself is trying to send us a message."

As if on cue, lightning struck a nearby hill with a deafening crack, splitting a tree in two. The group exchanged uneasy glances.

As the days went by, their unease deepened. Whispers began circulating through the villages—people were disappearing. At first, it was only a few isolated reports, but then it became more frequent. Farmers, hunters, even children had vanished, leaving no trace.

In one village, a distraught woman approached Kairos, her eyes red from crying. "My husband went into the woods two nights ago," she said, her voice trembling. "He said he saw... something moving between the trees, something dark. He never came back."

Kairos, Otona, and Gronkar immediately investigated, but they found no tracks, no signs of struggle—only the faintest impression of shadows that seemed to dart out of the corner of their eyes and vanish before they could be seen clearly. "It's like it's watching us," Otona whispered, her hand resting on the hilt of her dagger.

"I don't like this," Gronkar muttered. "It's too quiet. Too... unnatural."

Even the animals were affected. The once-peaceful creatures of the new lands were growing more unpredictable by the day. Birds, which had once filled the air with melodic songs, now flew in erratic patterns, swarming in chaotic clusters that scattered in all directions. Wolves, normally shy and elusive, had been spotted near the edge of settlements, their eyes glowing with an unsettling light.

During one patrol, a farmer approached them, breathless and pale. "Something's wrong with the animals. They're acting wild, crazed. The birds... the wolves... it's like they've gone mad."

Otona crouched beside the tracks of a wolf they had been tracking, her face grim. "It's the shapeshifter's influence. Even though we defeated it, something of its magic lingers."

Kairos nodded, his mind racing. "It's like the land is still infected by the shapeshifter's presence. We planted the Seed, but something... something dark is still holding on."

That night, the three of them sat by a fire, the glow flickering in the growing darkness. The air was thick with tension, and the weight of what they had seen that day hung heavily over them.

"It's not just the animals," Kairos said quietly, staring into the flames. "The land itself is wrong. Something is still here, still watching us."

Otona glanced at him, her eyes narrowing. "You think the shapeshifter isn't truly gone?"

Gronkar, usually so full of bravado, was unusually silent, his face set in a frown. "If it's gone, it sure left a mess behind."

Kairos ran his hand along the scar on his face, his thoughts heavy. "I don't know. But I can feel it. This isn't over. There's something we're missing, something we didn't stop."

Otona nodded. "We need to figure this out, before whatever it is gets stronger. Before more people disappear."

They all agreed. The shapeshifter had been defeated, but its shadow still lingered—an unseen threat that refused to leave, a darkness that seemed to be growing stronger with each passing day.

The group traveled to the outskirts of a remote village where the reports of disappearances had been particularly frequent. The air here was thick, the kind of silence that felt unnatural, as though the world itself was holding its breath. Otona led them deeper into the forest, her keen eyes scanning the ground for any clues. Gronkar, always wary, kept his weapon at the ready, while Kairos couldn't shake the feeling that they were walking into something far worse than what they had faced before.

The trail led them to a shadowed grove, one that seemed untouched by the healing magic of the Seed of Life. The trees here were twisted, their bark darkened and cracked as if something had sucked the life from them. Otona knelt down, her fingers brushing against the dirt. "There's something here," she whispered, eyes narrowing as she pointed to strange markings etched into the ground.

Kairos crouched beside her, studying the grooves in the earth. They were symbols—ancient runes, carved with precision, and radiating a faint, malevolent energy. "These are old," he muttered, "older than the shapeshifter. Older than anything we've encountered."

The runes pulsed faintly, and as Kairos reached out to touch one, a jolt of dark magic shot up his arm, causing him to pull back sharply.

"These symbols," Otona said, her voice barely above a whisper. "They're not just any magic. They're binding marks, used to control or contain something... something powerful."

Gronkar, peering over their shoulders, grunted. "If this is what controlled the shapeshifter, then we're in deeper trouble than we thought." He kicked at the ground, sending dirt scattering over the symbols. "Whatever put these here wasn't just playing around."

Kairos stood, feeling the weight of the discovery settling over him like a heavy cloak. "The shapeshifter wasn't acting alone. It was following orders, serving something—or someone—much older and more powerful." His voice grew grim as he looked at the twisting shadows around them. "We've been thinking too small. The shapeshifter wasn't the cause of this chaos; it was just another pawn in a much larger game."

The grove seemed to darken as if the land itself understood the weight of their realization. The wind howled through the trees, sending chills down their spines. Even Gronkar, who rarely flinched in the face of danger, looked uneasy.

Kairos stared at the runes, his mind racing. "This isn't over," he murmured. "Not by a long shot. We might have defeated the shapeshifter, but whatever put it in motion is still out there." He clenched his fists, frustration bubbling up inside him. "We're dealing with something far more ancient and far more dangerous than we realized."

Otona stood, her expression grim. "These runes aren't just remnants of the shapeshifter's magic. They're tied to something older. Something that has been waiting for its moment to rise."

Gronkar scowled, his grip tightening on his weapon. "We didn't come all this way to get caught up in another battle. But if something's out there, we need to know what we're up against."

The group shared a silent, uneasy glance. They had barely survived the shapeshifter's machinations, and now they faced the possibility that it was only the beginning of something much worse.

Kairos ran his hand over his scar as it pulsed faintly, a reminder that the darkness still lingered. "Whatever's coming," he said, "we need to be ready. This isn't just about the new lands anymore. It's about all of Mulvyon."

Otona nodded in agreement. "If these runes are tied to an ancient power, then we have to uncover the truth behind them. We need to understand what we're really facing."

Gronkar huffed, his expression hard. "I don't care how ancient or powerful it is. If it's coming for us, we'll be ready."

Despite Gronkar's bravado, the tension between them all was undeniable. They were no longer fighting to protect just the new lands—they were fighting to prevent something far darker from rising. The ancient power tied to these runes could unravel everything if it wasn't stopped.

As the group began to retrace their steps back toward the village, their minds were filled with thoughts of what lay ahead. The discovery of the ancient runes confirmed their worst fears: the shapeshifter was merely a symptom of a much larger disease. And that disease was spreading, its dark magic still clinging to the land, infecting everything it touched.

The group exchanged one final glance before leaving the shadowed grove behind, the weight of their discovery pressing down on their shoulders. The land might have been healing, but it was clear that its wounds were far deeper than they had imagined.

The sun hung low in the sky as Kairos, Otona, and Gronkar gathered near the edge of the restored lands. The Seed of Life had done its work, and the land was beginning to heal, but the group knew their journey was far from over. The strange occurrences—the shifting shadows, the runes, and the unnatural behavior of the creatures—spoke of something far darker still at play.

Kairos paced slowly, his hand absentmindedly tracing the scar that now ran across his face. He looked out at the horizon, where the new lands shimmered with their restored magic. "The shapeshifter was just the beginning," he said, his voice low but certain. "We've uncovered something much older and far more dangerous than we realized."

Otona leaned against a nearby tree, her bow slung over her shoulder. "These runes," she mused. "They're ancient, older than anything I've seen. They didn't just appear with the shapeshifter. There's something deeper here. Something that may have been waiting for the right moment to strike."

Gronkar grunted in agreement, his arms crossed over his chest. "We barely survived the shapeshifter. Whatever's coming next, we need to be ready. No more walking into this blind."

Kairos nodded, but his thoughts were clouded by uncertainty. "Is this where the shapeshifter came from?" he asked aloud. "Was it just a servant of a larger force?" The runes they'd discovered seemed to suggest as much. Something, or someone, had unleashed that darkness on Mulvyon, and now it was up to them to find out who or what was responsible.

"We need answers," Otona said. "This threat—it's bigger than the new lands. If these runes are any indication, we're dealing with something that could affect all of Mulvyon."

Kairos turned to face them both, his resolve hardening. "Then we leave the new lands. We need to find the source of this magic and uncover its connection to the shapeshifter. If there's a larger force at work, we can't afford to wait for it to come to us."

Gronkar cracked his knuckles, a grim smile tugging at the corners of his mouth. "I never thought we'd be off on another quest so soon, but if it means facing whatever's out there before it gets any stronger, I'm in."

The group fell into a contemplative silence, knowing that they were setting off into the unknown once more. The new lands had been saved, but the dark magic still lingered, and it would only be a matter of time before it threatened the rest of Mulvyon.

As they packed their belongings and prepared to leave, Kairos felt a strange mixture of hope and dread. The land they had fought so hard to save was healing, but what they had uncovered in the process suggested that their battles were far from over. The forces stirring beneath the surface of Mulvyon could be far greater than they had imagined, and they would need all their strength and wits to face what was coming.

"Whatever's out there," Kairos said quietly, "we'll face it together. But we need to be ready for anything."

Otona gave a curt nod, her eyes scanning the horizon. "The road ahead won't be easy. But we've faced impossible odds before."

Gronkar hefted his Warhammer onto his shoulder. "Let's hope this time we don't run into any more shapeshifters."

The three exchanged a brief smile, their camaraderie strengthened by the trials they had already endured. But as they set off into the distance, each of them knew that the danger ahead was far greater than anything they had faced before.

The wind whispered through the trees, carrying with it the faintest hint of something dark. Something watching. The new lands might have been saved, but Mulvyon's true battle was only just beginning.

Chapter 14

The midday sun bathed the new lands in warm light, but the mood of Kairos, Otona, and Gronkar was anything but calm. They worked tirelessly, coordinating the rebuilding efforts and helping villagers replant crops and restore homes. The scars of the battle against the shapeshifter were still raw, both in the land and in their hearts.

It was Gronkar who spotted her first. Standing at the edge of the tree line, Lethiriel watched them. Her piercing eyes, cold and calculating, took in everything. Kairos followed Gronkar's gaze, his heart sinking as he recognized the familiar figure. Otona's hand instinctively went to her bow, her entire body tensing at the sight of their nemesis.

Lethiriel stepped forward, her movements graceful and deliberate, as if she had no fear of what might happen next. The air between them was thick with tension.

"You should have known I'd return," Lethiriel said smoothly, her voice carrying with it an unsettling confidence. "The shapeshifter was never the true threat. You've only cut off one head of the beast."

Kairos clenched his fists, but he kept his voice measured. "What are you talking about, Lethiriel? You've betrayed us before, why should we trust anything you say?"

Lethiriel's lips curled into a slight smile. "Trust? No, I don't expect you to trust me. But I do expect you to listen if you want any hope of saving Mulvyon from what's coming."

Otona stepped forward, her voice sharp with suspicion. "You want us to believe you're here to help now? After everything you've done?" She didn't lower her bow, and Gronkar stood ready, his massive form tense.

Lethiriel's eyes flicked to Otona briefly before focusing on Kairos. "The shapeshifter was merely a servant of something far greater. It wasn't just chaos for the sake of chaos. Tythalor's rebellion was only part of the plan—an attempt to awaken something ancient. Something buried deep beneath Mulvyon. And it's stirring."

The words hung in the air, heavy and ominous. Kairos stared at her, his mind racing. "What are you saying? That Tythalor wasn't acting alone?"

Lethiriel's eyes glittered, and for the first time, there was a hint of something darker behind her composed demeanor. "Tythalor was ambitious, but he wasn't the mastermind. There's an ancient evil tied to the very foundations of this world—something that predates even the dragons. The shapeshifter was just a pawn in its game."

Otona's skepticism deepened. "And how would you know all of this, Lethiriel? What aren't you telling us?"

Lethiriel smiled again, this time more knowingly. "I've seen things. Learned things. While you were busy fighting the shapeshifter, I was gathering information—learning about the true nature of the threat we face. Tythalor's rebellion wasn't just about control; it was about release. The release of an ancient power that has slumbered for centuries."

Kairos felt a chill run down his spine. "So, you're saying that even with the shapeshifter gone, this... force is still out there?"

Lethiriel nodded, her gaze steady. "Yes. And now that the balance has been disturbed, it won't rest for long. It will rise again. But this time, it won't send a servant. It will come itself."

For a moment, there was silence, broken only by the rustle of the wind through the trees. Otona narrowed her eyes. "And what exactly do you plan to do about it, Lethiriel? If you knew all of this, why didn't you stop the shapeshifter yourself?"

Lethiriel's smile widened, but there was something unsettling in it. "Because I wasn't ready. Not yet. But now, with the shapeshifter defeated, I have a better understanding of what we're dealing with. This power... it's not something that can be destroyed. But it can be controlled."

Kairos felt a surge of unease. There was a gleam in Lethiriel's eyes that hadn't been there before—an ambition, a hunger. "What are you saying?"

Lethiriel stepped closer, her voice lowering to a near whisper. "What I'm saying, Kairos, is that this power could reshape Mulvyon. It could bring about a new order—a world where we control the magic, not the other way around. But to do that, we'll need to unlock its full potential. I've already begun to understand it. Together, we could harness it."

Kairos recoiled, the scar on his face burning as if in response to her words. He glanced at Otona and Gronkar, both of whom were watching Lethiriel with a mixture of suspicion and anger.

"We're not interested in playing with dark magic, Lethiriel," Kairos said firmly. "We came to restore balance, not to gain control."

Lethiriel's smile didn't falter, but there was a shadow of something darker behind her eyes. "We'll see," she said softly. "The world is changing, and soon you'll realize that sometimes, control is the only way to survive."

With that, she turned and disappeared back into the shadows, leaving the group unsettled and unsure of what lay ahead.

The group stood in uneasy silence after Lethiriel's cryptic departure. The dark magic that had once swirled in the new lands seemed to echo in her words. Kairos, his hand still resting on the hilt of his dagger, struggled to process what she had said. Otona remained tense, her gaze fixed on the spot where Lethiriel had disappeared. Gronkar, ever the pragmatist, stood with his arms crossed, his brow furrowed in deep thought.

Moments later, Lethiriel reappeared, slipping out of the shadows like a ghost. There was something unnervingly calm about her demeanor, and the group instinctively recoiled as she approached, her eyes gleaming with unsettling knowledge.

"I see you're still processing my words," she said smoothly, her voice carrying the same confidence as before. "But this is just the beginning. You don't understand the full scope of what you're dealing with."

Kairos's scar throbbed faintly, a reminder of their last encounter with the shapeshifter. He forced himself to stand tall, his voice steady but wary. "You said the shapeshifter was just a servant. What do you mean by that?"

Lethiriel's smile was thin and sharp. "The shapeshifter was never the true threat. It was merely a tool—a puppet, if you will—of something far older, far more dangerous. The real enemy has been buried beneath Mulvyon for centuries, waiting for the right moment to awaken. It feeds on chaos, on instability. Tythalor's rebellion, the chaos that followed—it was all part of its grand design."

Otona stepped forward, her eyes narrowing. "And how do you know all of this, Lethiriel? What are you not telling us?"

Lethiriel's expression darkened slightly, but she didn't falter. "I've studied the old texts, the ancient runes buried deep within the forgotten places of Mulvyon. While you were fighting the shapeshifter, I was learning the truth about the power that lies beneath this world. It's older than dragons, older than the magic that shaped Mulvyon itself. And now that the balance has been shattered, it stirs once more."

Gronkar let out a frustrated growl, his eyes locked on Lethiriel. "And what exactly do you want with this power? Don't try to tell us you're here just to help."

Lethiriel's smile didn't reach her eyes. "I'm not foolish enough to let that kind of power go unchecked. But I also know that such a force cannot simply be destroyed. It's woven into the very fabric of Mulvyon. If we're going to stop it from destroying everything, we need to understand it, and perhaps... guide it."

Her words sent a chill through the group. There was an almost reverential tone in her voice, as if she saw the ancient entity as more than just a threat. Kairos could feel the undercurrent of ambition running through her words, like a dark current just beneath the surface.

Otona's voice was sharp, cutting through the tension. "Guide it? You're talking about controlling it, aren't you?"

Lethiriel's eyes flashed with something unreadable. "Control is a strong word. But if we're to survive what's coming, we need to be smart. The entity isn't just a mindless force of destruction. It has purpose, and with the right influence, that purpose can be shaped."

Kairos took a step forward, his gaze hardening. "You're playing with fire, Lethiriel. We've seen what happens when someone tries to control dark magic. It corrupts. It destroys."

For the first time, Lethiriel's smile faded, replaced by something darker. "Perhaps," she said quietly. "But that power is inevitable. You think you can simply defeat it with brute strength? You're wrong. It's too deeply ingrained in this world, too ancient to be cast aside like the shapeshifter. If you truly want to save Mulvyon, you'll need to understand that. Sometimes, survival means bending the rules."

Kairos felt a shiver run down his spine. There was a dangerous gleam in Lethiriel's eyes, an ambition that went far beyond stopping this ancient force. It was clear to him now—Lethiriel wasn't just here to fight the darkness. She wanted to control it, to wield it for her own ends. And that made her just as dangerous as the force they were facing.

"You think you can control it," Kairos said, his voice low. "But you're wrong. Power like that can't be harnessed. It will consume you."

Lethiriel tilted her head, her expression unreadable. "We'll see," she said softly. "But I think you'll find that sometimes the only way to win is to play the game better than your opponent."

Her words hung in the air, the unspoken threat lingering like a shadow over the group. Kairos glanced at Otona and Gronkar, both of whom looked equally uneasy. There was no doubt in his mind now—Lethiriel was dangerous, not just because of what she knew, but because of what she wanted.

"Whatever you're planning," Kairos said, his voice firm, "we're not interested. We'll find our own way to stop this."

Lethiriel raised an eyebrow, her smile returning. "I expected nothing less from you, Kairos. But when the time comes, and you realize you can't win this war without me, I'll be waiting."

The group stood in tense silence as Lethiriel's words lingered in the air. The weight of her offer pressed heavily on Kairos, Otona, and Gronkar. The prospect of uncovering the truth about the dark force beneath Mulvyon was tempting, but the danger of trusting Lethiriel—who had already betrayed them before—was a risk they could not ignore.

Lethiriel's gaze flicked between them, her voice smooth and persuasive. "You've seen what's happening in the new lands. The instability isn't just a byproduct of the shapeshifter's defeat. This force is ancient, and it's already begun to stretch its influence. If you want to save Mulvyon, you'll need to face it head-on." She took a step forward, her eyes narrowing slightly as she spoke with conviction. "But you won't succeed without me. I know where to begin. I know how to find the origin of this darkness."

Kairos clenched his fists, his mind racing. He knew she wasn't entirely wrong—they lacked the knowledge to stop this ancient evil, and Lethiriel had proven that she possessed a deeper understanding of the dark magic that plagued their world. But trusting her felt like stepping into a trap.

Otona crossed her arms, her sharp eyes never leaving Lethiriel. "You've already shown us who you are, Lethiriel," she said coldly. "You can't be trusted. This is just another one of your schemes, and I'm not going to let you drag us into whatever power play you're making."

Gronkar grunted, sharing Otona's skepticism. "You betrayed us before. Why should we trust you now? For all we know, you're just trying to use us to get closer to this power."

Lethiriel smiled, a hint of amusement flickering in her eyes. "I don't expect blind trust," she admitted. "But what I offer is the only path forward. You've seen the runes, the signs. There's something much bigger than the shapeshifter at work here. If we don't stop it now, it will consume everything. The new lands, Mulvyon, everything you've fought for—it will all be undone." Her voice was measured, carefully crafted to stoke their fear and ambition.

Kairos, still silent, felt the weight of the decision settling on his shoulders. His scar throbbed as he recalled the battle with the shapeshifter. If what Lethiriel said was true—if the entity that empowered the shapeshifter was still out there, lurking beneath Mulvyon—then they had to act. But Lethiriel's motives were too murky, too dangerous to ignore.

Otona stepped closer to Kairos, her voice low but firm. "You can't seriously be considering this, Kairos. She's manipulating us, trying to twist our fear into some kind of power grab. We can't trust her."

Gronkar nodded in agreement, though his expression was more conflicted. "Otona's right. We've come this far without her, and we can keep going. But she's offering something we don't have—information."

Lethiriel took a step back, her eyes glinting with ambition as she addressed the group. "I won't deny that I want this power under control," she said, her voice silkier than before. "It can't be left unchecked. But that doesn't mean we have to let it destroy us. If we find its source, we can stop it... or direct it." She smiled faintly, her gaze locking onto Kairos. "Imagine a world where we don't just stop the darkness, but reshape it to serve us. To remake Mulvyon into something stronger."

Kairos's heart pounded as he considered her words. Her subtle suggestion that the dark force could be controlled—wielded even—filled him with a mix of dread and curiosity. She spoke of saving Mulvyon, but he could sense the hunger for power beneath her rhetoric. Yet, the thought gnawed at him. Could they really defeat this ancient evil without understanding its origins? And did they even have the time to go down this path with Lethiriel?

Otona's hand gripped his arm, pulling him out of his thoughts. "This is dangerous, Kairos. She's already made it clear that she's after power. We can't let her manipulate us into making a deal with the devil."

Kairos met Otona's gaze, knowing she was right. But still, there was something undeniable about the situation. Lethiriel held knowledge they desperately needed. If they refused her help, they might be leaving Mulvyon to face a darkness they didn't fully understand.

Finally, he spoke, his voice quiet but resolute. "We don't have to trust her," he said, his eyes on Lethiriel, "but we need answers. We'll follow her lead for now, but on our terms."

Lethiriel's smile widened. "A wise choice, Kairos. You'll see—this is the only way forward."

Otona stepped back, frustration flashing in her eyes, but she didn't protest further. Gronkar remained silent, his jaw clenched as he considered their precarious position. None of them were happy with the decision, but they knew they were walking a thin line.

Kairos felt the knot in his stomach tighten, knowing they had just set foot on a dangerous path. One where Lethiriel's ambitions might lead them toward something darker than they could imagine. And he wasn't sure if they would be able to pull back when the time came.

The air was thick with tension as the group made their final preparations to leave the new lands. Though the chaos caused by the shapeshifter had subsided, a sense of unease still hung over them, more palpable now with Lethiriel's presence. The decision had been made—they would follow her, but not without doubt gnawing at the back of their minds.

Otona adjusted the straps on her bow, her sharp eyes watching Lethiriel from a distance. "I still don't trust her," she muttered, her voice low but firm. "She's using us again."

Kairos stood beside her; his brow furrowed in thought. He could sense the mistrust radiating from Otona and Gronkar, and even within himself, the doubts stirred. "We don't have a choice," he said quietly. "She knows things we don't. And if what she says about this dark force is true, we're running out of time."

Gronkar grunted as he sharpened his axe, the scrape of metal against stone punctuating his frustration. "It's not the first time we've walked into danger. She's hiding something—more than we realize."

Lethiriel stood a short distance away, her posture relaxed but her expression unreadable. She seemed to sense the tension, but instead of acknowledging it, she pressed forward with a quiet confidence that unsettled them all.

The group gathered what little supplies they had left, knowing this journey would take them far beyond familiar territory. The new lands, once chaotic and ravaged, were slowly healing thanks to the Seed of Life. But the scars of the battle remained, not only on the land but in their hearts.

"Do you think we'll ever see this place again?" Gronkar asked, his tone gruff, though there was a hint of something deeper—perhaps a quiet hope that one day, they would return to see the land fully restored.

Kairos shrugged; his gaze fixed on the horizon. "If we don't stop what's coming, it won't matter. The new lands will fall like everything else."

Otona glanced toward the distance, her expression softening for just a moment. "We did our part here. But if this force is real... there's more at stake than just these lands."

As the group finished packing, Lethiriel moved to the front, her movements graceful but deliberate. "It's time," she said, her voice calm but with an undercurrent of something more—something almost triumphant. "The journey ahead will take us into Mulvyon's hidden past, to places forgotten by time. But the answers you seek are there."

Otona narrowed her eyes, watching Lethiriel closely. "And what answers are you looking for?"

Lethiriel smiled faintly, her gaze shifting to the distant mountains. "The truth, Otona. The truth that will reshape this world."

As the group set off, there was a noticeable shift in the air. Lethiriel's stride was purposeful, as though she was already on the path toward something she had long sought. Her confidence was unnerving, leaving the group with the sinking feeling that they weren't just following her—they were playing right into her hands.

Kairos felt the weight of their decision pressing down on him as they walked. He couldn't shake the sense that they were being drawn into something much bigger, something far darker than even the shapeshifter. Lethiriel had made it clear that this ancient evil could be controlled, but at what cost?

As they moved deeper into the unknown, Kairos glanced at Otona and Gronkar, the silent promise between them unspoken—they would face whatever came together, even if it meant standing against Lethiriel when the time came.

But deep down, Kairos wondered: Could they stop her, if it came to that?

The new lands slowly disappeared behind them as Kairos, Otona, Gronkar, and Lethiriel ventured further through Mulvyon. While walking the air was thick with an unnatural energy—an oppressive force that seemed to coil around them as they traveled. The sun barely pierced through the thick clouds that gathered on the horizon, casting everything in a cold, gray light.

As the group left the new lands behind, the air grew thick with tension. Unnatural phenomena followed them—mutated creatures with twisted forms lurked in the shadows, and the skies shifted from dark clouds to violent storms. It was clear that the dark magic beneath Mulvyon was stirring, growing stronger with each step they took.

THE SHAPESHIFTER'S WRATH

Lethiriel walking ahead of the group with unsettling confidence. Her gaze was fixed on the distance, and every now and then, she would hint at the growing darkness. "This power... it can be controlled," she said, almost to herself, though her voice carried back to the group. The implication was clear—Lethiriel wasn't just guiding them to stop the ancient evil. She had other plans.

Kairos glanced at Otona and Gronkar, both of whom shared his unease. Otona, ever-watchful, whispered, "She wants more than just to stop this. She thinks she can harness it."

Gronkar nodded, his hand tightening around his weapon. "We'll need to watch her."

As they pressed on, the land continued to shift around them, reacting to the rising darkness beneath. Though the shapeshifter was gone, the true threat was awakening, and the group could feel its presence closing in.

Milton Keynes UK
Ingram Content Group UK Ltd.
UKHW042002281024
450365UK00003B/113